monsoonbooks

MY KIASU TEENAGE

After growing up in Malaysia _____ __n See
graduated from the University of C_ _____ ___rently lives in
New York, where she works on W__ ____ day and runs a teen
mentoring program, Chumz (www.chu ___.net), in her spare time. Ee Lin
claims to have read over 400 books by Enid Blyton.

Ee Lin's email is eelinsee@gmail.com and she loves to hear from her
readers.

MY KIASU TEENAGE LIFE IN SINGAPORE

by ae lin see

To Nat

A peek into the life of a
teenager living in singapore
for you !!   :)

Love,
Aunty susan
1.1.06

monsoon

monsoonbooks

Published in 2005
by Monsoon Books Pte Ltd
Blk 106 Jalan Hang Jebat #02–14
Singapore 139527
www.monsoonbooks.com.sg

ISBN 981-05-3016-1

Cover design by Lynn Teo

Printed in Singapore

10 09 08 07 06 05   1 2 3 4 5 6 7 8 9

For Mom, who bought me marshmallows
so that I could see what they were and made me scones,
and Dad, who taught me Christmas carols
and made egg-heads from plaster with me.
Thank you for giving me a wonderful childhood in Malaysia.

kiasu *Hokkien* (kja:su:) ADJECTIVE scared to lose, competitive

Contents

Characters in Pei Yi's World

Best friend
Mei Yee

Family
Mum and Dad
Yi Hoon (sister)
Lolo and Bimbo (cats)

Hostel friends (Malaysians)

New girls	Existing girls
Jen Nee (CHIJ, Sec 3)	Betty (CHIJ, Sec 4)
Alisa the beautiful one (CHIJ, Sec 3)	Nancy (CHIJ, Sec 3)
Elizabeth the smart one (RGS, Sec3)	Pau Leen (RGS, Sec 3)
Sunny (RGS, Sec 3)	Nicole (CHIJ, Sec 2, roommate)

Hostel guys
Ekan
Matt
Cheng Hoe the scientific one
Gaik Teong the crazy one
Leo the disgusting one
Niles (Pau Leen's brother)
Eric (Alvin the Chipmunk)

Hostel enemy
Miss Lily Sim

CHIJ classmates (Singaporeans)
Yoonphaik
Lingling
Huiwee

Glossary

Sec 1–4 Secondary 1–4 (age 13–17)
JC 1–2 Junior College 1–2 (age 18–19)
CHIJ Convent of the Holy Infant Jesus
RGS Raffles Girls' School

1
Wish You Were Here

Friday 27 December

Dearest Mei Yee
It's now 9.30 pm and I'm with my dad in the bus on the way to Singapore! Thinking of things I want to tell you all the time. Leaving BM at the age of 15 ... Wonder if I'll survive the *kiasu* environment there.
Love, Pei Yi

Saturday 28 December (*First day in Singapore*)

Dearest Mei Yee
I'm finally in Singapore! It's now 6.30 pm at Hua Zhong Hostel. I'm feeling miserable, lonely and lost. I'm staying in the hostel with other Malaysian students but we all attend Singaporean schools. Wish you were here as my roommate. I've just taken two photos of my room to show you what it looks like. The left half of the room is mine. The other side belongs to a Sec 2 ASEAN scholar named Nicole, who has been here for a year. She speaks English with a British accent. How intimidating. She has very long hair and she's bigger and taller than me.

Glossary
kiasu Hokkien scared to lose, competitive
BM Bukit Mertajam, a small town in the state of Penang, Malaysia
ASEAN scholar The scholarship is given by the Singapore government to students from ASEAN (Association of South East Asian Nations) countries to study in Singapore

---

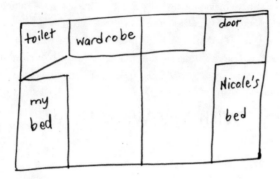

The girl who lives next door is Jen Nee, she's also from Penang.

We get to choose whether we go to a Science class or an Arts class. I'm going to choose Class 3A4 (3 Arts 4). The subjects are English, Malay, Elementary Maths, Additional Maths, English Literature, History, Physics (!!) and Accounts. My dad would rather me take Chemistry instead of Physics but I want Physics. Oh dear, I don't know what games to take. They have tennis, swimming, netball, ping-pong etc, but I can't play any of them.

In the afternoon, my dad and I went to Toa Payoh where my school is. I saw so many teenagers with Walkmans! Like they're under water and the Walkman is the oxygen tank. I bought my uniform—two pinafores and three white blouses—for S$58.10. Expensive!!

I haven't really seen my school yet. Just caught a glimpse when the bus passed it. I'll take a photo and you can compare it with the scene in your dream.

It's still Saturday, 9.40 pm. The girls are all really nice—fun, friendly, crazy—but I really miss you. After dinner, we sat on the stairs and chitchatted and joked. Then I started thinking of you and cried in front of everyone. So I came up to my room on the first floor. My nose is so blocked I can't breathe. My dad is in a hotel, I don't know which one.

The girls I've met so far are Betty (Sec 4), Nicole (my roommate), Pau Leen (Sec 3)—are all Chinese from Malaysia. They're all old scholars (meaning they've stayed at the hostel for more than a year, but may have come in Sec 1). They've done all sorts of crazy stuff like climbing into each other's rooms through windows. They matchmake each other with guys. No one really studies hard at all! They're a bunch of crazy girls and don't really follow rules. There's going to be a Signature Hunt, where the newcomers have to ask the seniors for their signatures, and the seniors will ask them to do all sorts of crazy and embarrassing stuff like proposing to guys and hugging someone's leg.

The hostel consists of three blocks, four stories each. I'm in Block A. Block B is for guys (been introduced to some but can't remember their names), Block C is for wardens and Junior College students. I've accidentally gone up the boy's block twice and even fitted my key into the keyhole of Room 201 of Block B. The prep room where we're supposed to study under supervision is air-conned. My roommate is being so nice to me 'coz my eyes are really red with crying.

Glossary
first floor second floor in the United States. In Asia, the stories of a building are ground floor, first floor, second floor, etc.
air-conned air-conditioned

Have you heard of the word Singlish (Singapore English)? Here are some words that people use a lot:

   kiasuism from the word *kiasu* (scared to lose). *Kiasu* is like the
      national word here. They even have Mr Kiasu, a cartoon character.
   mugger toad someone who studies a lot
   blur look confused, not alert
   stone to have an expressionless face
   sabo short for sabotage (an activity commonly practised in the
      hostel!)
   leh often used at the end of the sentence instead of *lah*

I heard that some of the girls go back to Malaysia for Chinese New Year so I'll go back too. I wonder when I'll adapt to life here and become "one of the girls". Oh ya, I haven't seen any really cute guys. I can't have a crush when I'm so miserable. I want to phone you now but if I do, I'll start crying and won't be able to talk. OK, I'm going to write to my sister now. My address: Hua Zhong Hostel, 673 Bukit Timah Road, Singapore 1026. I can't receive personal calls; only messages when you phone the office. Actually, after listening to all the stories of the girls I know it's a LOT of fun staying in a hostel. It's just that I wish you were here.

Hey, keep my letters properly!! Don't leave them on the table or in between books.
Love, Pei Yi

Sunday 29 December (*Second day in Singapore*)

Dearest Mei Yee

After breakfast, the girls and I went to the lounge where we joked and talked. They told a lot of dirty jokes, which I'm going to add to my collection and tell you when I get back.

Then my dad came and we went to Toa Payoh and had lunch. I bought white shoes (you know, the kind with sharp toes) for Orientation. First time I'll be wearing this kind of shoes. They're not high-heeled. S$14.90. The girls here are those you'll probably get used to and joke with sooner or later but not those you get close to. I doubt if I'll find a close friend. You don't talk heart-to-heart with them like you and me do, you know. I always thought people studying in Singapore study like hell but these people I've met fool around and don't abide by the rules. Maybe it's 'coz school hasn't started. So how's school back in BM?

I get to watch the six o'clock show *The Blood of Good & Evil* too! It's a great life here, actually; if only you were here. So far I've written to you and Yi Hoon. I've only been here two days and I miss you already. It's funny, you know, some weekends I didn't see you when I was in BM, and I haven't seen you for only two days. Please write to me often. I'll check the letter rack for letters everyday.

My dad will go back on Tuesday.
Love, Pei Yi

Tuesday 31 December

Dearest Mei Yee
I'm reading a *Sweet Valley High* book that belongs to Nicole.

When will you be coming to Singapore? You can't stay at my hostel unless you pay S$14/night. I can't wait to see you again. I wish I wasn't such an emotional person.

A lot of girls here are going to CHIJ (my school, Convent of the Holy Infant Jesus). A few are going to RGS (Raffles Girls School). I haven't met any who are taking Arts—they are all taking Science—but Betty (Sec 4) said she wished she'd taken Arts. Nothing is really strict here, actually. There're no rankings in class too.

> **Glossary**
> **convent** Catholic school for girls, not where you go to learn to be a nun!

Betty is very friendly and funny. She wears contact lenses 'coz her power in each eye is over 800! She said Singaporean girls in school are the people you can talk to (like joke and small talk) but not get close to. I think I'll probably be lonely in class and be labelled quiet and all. Actually I don't really want to get close to anyone here. No, I guess I do want to have a close friend here. Everyone (the seniors) seems to be close to one another and I'm rather lonely.

I read your star (Capricorn) today. It says something about you inviting some friends over to your house this week or something. Mine is horrible—about unlucky stuff in the beginning of the week!

Reply soon, please!
Love, Pei Yi

Tuesday 31st December (*Second letter today!*)

Dearest Mei Yee
Yesterday, I got to know Alisa (a pretty Eurasian-looking girl—she's actually pure Chinese) and Jen Nee better. Alisa is sooo beautiful, she has a good, clear and fair complexion, long, slightly wavy hair and a great body. She's quite muscular too! The bridge of her nose is high, which is why she looks like she's a Eurasian. Jen Nee is cute-looking, like a puppy. She really makes me laugh!

This morning, my dad took Jen Nee and I to have our x-rays taken. I slept at 1.30 am yesterday and I'm sleepy now. It's raining now, has been raining everyday. Have you ever taken x-ray? The robe you get into is so thin. It's awkward 'coz you can't wear a bra.

We went to CHIJ today. I think it's like your dream—side gate, trees and all!!!!! It's confirmed—I'm going to Sec 3A4. Even though it's an Arts class, I'll still be learning Physics. I'm the first ASEAN scholar to join 3A4. Usually they go to Science 1, S2, S3 or Arts 1, but I prefer the subject combination in A4. No one in my hostel is in that class. Sister Elaine, my headmistress, was the nun at my scholarship interview! She has an incredible memory. She remembers me and remembers everyone's results! She is very petite and frail but there's an aura around her that makes people respect her. My dad didn't dare to ask too many questions 'coz she can really scare people. The school is nice. Actually everything here is very advanced and nice.

Just now all of us (about 15 of us) went to Nancy's room. We joked and laughed. I enjoyed listening to the jokes very much. The "baby jokes" were SO funny. I've got to tell you all of them when I get back. Here's one: What's gross? Seven dead babies in a can. What's grosser? A dead baby in seven cans. Another one: What's gross? A live baby with dead babies in a car. What's grosser? The live baby eating its way out. What's grossest? The live baby coming back for second helping!

Everyone has her own way of talking. Jen Nee likes to say, "Like ..." in front of every sentence or "sort of" so often. I hope I don't catch it. Jen Nee is like me in some ways—she can't remember timetables in school (what class is when), she's bad at directions and, in Penang, when she was in a floating class (where each class is held in a different classroom) she didn't know where to go. She just followed her classmates. Like me.

I haven't looked through my textbooks yet, too lazy. I spend most of my time writing to you or going here and there.

The food here is so good! I didn't really watch the six o'clock show just now—I was eating and sitting too far away to see properly.

Sometimes my dad too overworried about me. It irritates me sometimes, but later I feel sorry for being irritated.

I'm having social problems. You know what I mean? Everyone (I mean the seniors) seems so sociable and close to each other. Oh ya, when I say "seniors" I mean those who've stayed in Hua Zhong for a year or more, but may be Sec 2, 3 or 4. If you were here, I'd really love it. I think the teachers will be really good, 'coz they have to be.

I feel quite lost in Singapore. The buildings and roads and all are confusing. Everything here is so clean. They fine you for littering, even for dropping a small piece of paper on the ground. I saw this t-shirt that says, "Singapore is a Fine City." But I'm very impressed with how efficient and posh everything is! Oh ya, there is a law against selling chewing gum here, but we're allowed to bring small quantities in if it's not for resale. At the MRT station, there is a sign with a picture of a durian and a not-permitted sign on it, because durians will stink up the MRT.

In CHIJ they have AEP (Art Elective Program) where a foreigner comes to teach. Betty said the teacher was saying he's bringing a male model (NAKED!) for them but didn't. AEP sounds fun. I might take it. All the clubs sound nice—I feel like taking them all but I can choose only one so maybe I'll choose Choir. Photography sounds nice.
Love, Pei Yi

Glossary
durian tropical fruit with a thorny rind and a pungent smell
MRT Mass Rapid Transit, Singapore's railway system

Tuesday 31 December (*Third letter today!!*)

Dearest Mei Yee
Last day of the year! In the morning, we had a briefing. The people from MOE (Ministry of Education) gave us talks, then the seniors sang for us. We had food and were supposed to mingle around and get to know ASEAN scholars from other hostels too. Then, Pau Leen, Jen Nee and I went to buy textbooks. We had lunch, then went to Coro (short for Coronation Plaza; another abb; abb=abb for abbreviation). Coro is a shopping centre very close to our hostel. There's a nice grocery store on the ground floor and lots of different stores upstairs, like bookstores, music stores, gift stores and pet food stores. Bought S$12 worth of 30cent stamps. I spent time reading birthday cards while they bought textbooks. I saw some huge cards (as big as two TV sets)—very funny and they only cost S$14!

Pau Leen has a lot of jokes to tell—I love jokes. I've copied quite a few in my diary. There are a lot of pretty and smart girls here.

I like drawing robins; I got the idea from a Christmas card. I love reading funny cards and *Archie* comics.

I keep wishing you were here. My dad went back today.

No letters for me at all—how disappointing.
Love, Pei Yi

Wednesday 1 January!!!

Dearest Mei Yee
Phoned you this morning. So nice to talk to you!

We played basketball today. I'm not good at it but it was OK fun. I'm writing to you while watching the six o'clock show. The TV's blur.

I like some of my hostelites very much: Pau Leen, Nancy, Betty and Jen Nee to name a few. Some of the seniors stayed at Orchard Road from last night until 7 am this morning! They went bowling. Orchard Road is the posh street that you see on TV with all the Christmas lights during Christmas. All the stores are huge and very expensive! Teenagers like to hang out there, especially at the cinemas.

I told Jen Nee about my friends in BM, especially about you. You know, I won't accept the truth if I don't like it. Like, everyone tells me that when I come to Singapore and stay so far away from you, we won't be as close as before anymore. Maybe it's true but I just won't accept it.

The seniors were shocked that I like the hostel food. My tray was eaten so clean that Betty brought some of her friends to see it! Like my tray is a piece of art or something. It's so disappointing not to receive any letters. I check the letter racks about twice a day.

Love, Pei Yi

Thursday 2 January

Dear Mei Yee

I'm now in CHIJ. It's 9.15 am. No lessons yet. I'm the only ASEAN scholar in my class. At the beginning of today, I was miserable, quiet, lonely and scared 'coz I felt lonely in class. I'm quite lost in school (I mean my sense of direction). Some people in my school puff out their uniforms at the chest and some wear their belts at their hips.

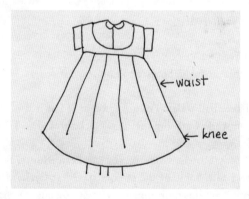

Hi! It's 2.30 pm. I'm back from school. School dismisses at 1.20 pm. I'm beginning to enjoy it. Our form teacher is Mrs Simons. My classmates are nice. There's a very friendly girl who looks very cute. Her name is Yoonphaik.

Our lessons are very interesting. The teachers are very interesting; they

teach properly. Well, that's my impression of school after the first day ...
Our Add. Maths teacher is nice. Our history teacher is a Eurasian.
Sometimes she takes her students to Malaysia or Java to see what they're
learning. She said we might go to Penang this year.

The canteen food is so damn expensive. I ate delicious *wonton mee*.
I want to join Choir. They sing Latin songs and sing in parts.

Our history is only about Malaysia and Singapore. Sigh! We have to
write three-page essays for exam—you would be good at that. We did
have some lessons today. Oh ya, I'm doing Combined Physics &
Chemistry, not Pure Physics or Pure Chem. The Physics I learn is easier
than the Science classes'.

Tomorrow, I'm taking a drawing test to see if I can take AEP. I really,
really hope I'll be accepted to take AEP! They have free trips to Europe,
America and Japan. They teach pottery, jewellery design, textile design,
art criticism, art history, photography and art appreciation, and they
have trips to buildings, art galleries, museums and art exhibitions. The
teachers are really qualified and are from overseas. Only four schools in
Singapore have this programme. But this programme is very difficult and
we have to take it for O levels if we study it.

Alisa has a lot of admirers from my hostel and other hostels. Nicole is
very *manja*. Sometimes she flaps her arms. I still have homework but I'm
going to read *Archie* comics.

I'm a bit famous for eating everything on my tray during meals.

REPLY SOON! REPLY MORE!
Love, Pei Yi

Glossary
manja *Malay* to act in a cute, coy or teasing manner

Friday 3 January

Dearest Mei Yee

I've just taken the AEP test. There were two papers, half an hour each. For the first paper, we drew our hand holding something and for the other paper, we drew a building. I can't draw buildings.

There are a lot of cute and colourful posters pinned on my school walls everywhere; most of them are the societies' campaigns for inviting members. The art room is full of all sorts of creative things. Some pop art and all very colourful. Also sculpture. There was a life-size dummy that looked like a mummy and it scared me to death. I thought it was a dead person or something.

The room where we learn Malay is air-conned. For Eng. Lit. we read a love poem by Shakespeare. The teacher is nice.

My classmates aren't as good at Maths as I thought they would be, fortunately. My Maths teacher, Mrs Simons (she's Chinese but married to an *ang moh*) is very good at teaching.

> **Glossary**
> *ang moh* Hokkien a Caucasian person, literally red hair

Slept the whole afternoon, read *Archie* and broke my alarm clock. I read *Teenage* magazine and also *Teen* at night.

Your lucky day—30 Jan; the horoscope says your family will be an important aspect of your life this month.

I read an article in the papers today about a pair of seven-year-old twins in Penang who have a disease, progeria or something, that makes them age quickly. Their sizes are like four year olds but they are balding and dying fast.

Jen Nee's roommate is not an ASEAN scholar. She's just rich. She pays S$4000 a year for the hostel, S$3000 as a "donation" to Singapore, S$2000 to her school and S$57 a month in school fees! Singapore makes a lot of money through its education system!

I wonder how many bricks were used to build my house, or this hostel?

I haven't touched my homework at all today.
Love, Pei Yi

Sunday 5 January

Dearest Mei Yee

Why don't you write to me?? I just came back from Beauty World where we (nine of us) had lunch and then shopped. I'm locked out of my room 'coz I forgot to take out my keys and I can't find Nicole. We thought the name Beauty World was so funny, like we're going there to become beautiful, but actually it's just a very normal shopping complex. It's actually quite old. There's a huge foodcourt on the top floor with tons of different food stalls, almost like the hawker centres in Malaysia.

There was a machine there where you insert 40 cents and choose from four colours: red, blue, green and yellow. You arrange them according to the colour you like the most and the machine analyses your selection and tells you your character. It says I'm spontaneous and trusting and some-times easily fooled. It also said I want to be famous. Everyone laughed.

I bought Chicken In A Biskit, Indomee, potato chips, a notebook and a file. I'm famous for my appetite.

Glossary
hawker centre a foodcourt with many individually owned stalls each selling a type of food
Chicken in a Biskit a brand of chicken-flavoured biscuits
Indomee a popular brand of instant noodles

Pau Leen is so cute and funny. She looks like the Abominable Snowman in one of the jokes and when she smiles, her rows of white teeth are so cute. When she smiles, you can see two rectangular rows of teeth! I'm going to take a photo of her to show you. She's quite tomboyish and very disciplined! She's also very fit and muscular and plays tennis and tons of other sports.

Yesterday was real fun! We and some other people from another hostel (CJC Hostel) went to East Coast Park. Have you been there? There're nice bike paths to cycle on. I rented a mountain bike and cycled a very long distance. We had a Signature Hunt, which was fun. I had to propose to so many people, and do other embarrassing stuff: kneel down, hold a guy's hand, walk around hand-in-hand with a guy and announce we're newly married, say "You've nice hips and a cheeky face" to five guys and hold their hips and pinch their faces ... Some girls had to slow-dance with guys. There are over 80 names on the list and I've got only about 19 of their signatures. Three weeks more to do it. We also played three games—very, really, really fun!!

I've received my swimsuit and letters from my family. I phone home every week. My dad made a list of advice for me:

    1 Focus on your priorities: safety, health, studies
    2 Look right, then left, then right again before crossing the road
    3 See the doctor immediately if you get sick
    4 Study hard (do well in Maths)
    5 Keep warm at night
    6 Bring an umbrella when you go out in case it rains
    7 Eat fruits and vegetables

We've all been so lazy!! I haven't studied at all. Read a dirty book. My new friends know I'm dirty-minded already.

Glossary

dirty book romance book like Harlequin books, not pornography!

We call RI (Raffles' Institution, the top school in Singapore): Retarded Institution; while the guys call my school CHIJ: Crazy Hypocrites, Idiotic Jerks! Ha! Ha! Ha!

Love, Pei Yi

Monday 6 January

Dear Mei Yee

Yippee!! I got into AEP!! So happy. Jen Nee, Alisa and Nancy also got in. Jen Nee was worried about the art history part 'coz it's quite difficult. We have to write essays and stuff. Mr Como (AEP teacher) said it's good to know art history 'coz when you go to formal functions or art galleries with high-class people, they always talk about art and music.

I'm now in the prep room (I have prep from 7.30 to 9.30 pm). It's air-conned, and for each person there are three boards on top of the table, one in front of you, two on the sides. We call it a hutch. Pau Leen sits beside me. I took a photo of her to show you. She grinned the Abominable Snowman grin for the photo.

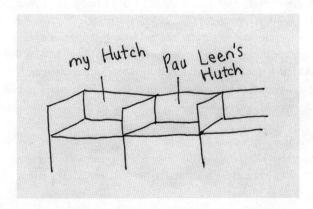

Yesterday, for signature hunt, Betty made me slow-dance with a guy named Cheng Hoe. It was embarrassing. He dared not put his hands on my waist. He said he had never touched a girl before. He looks like the

27

very *kuai* kind of guy but he can actually be quite good looking. Then Betty made me go up to the first floor and shout down, "Cheng Hoe, I love you! Marry me!" Two years ago, Pau Leen was awarded first prize for Signature Hunt for getting the most signatures and for being a good sport.

Glossary

kuai Hokkien obedient, decent, a goody-goody

I received your letter today. I was so happy. I check the office three or four times a day for letters. I read your letter and started crying and laughing at the same time. Alisa and Nancy were laughing at me laughing and crying, like I was mad or something.

OK, now to reply to your letter. How many letters from me have you received? It's funny if you receive some and you write to me while I'm writing to you and you haven't received them. I kept laughing hysterically while reading your letter. I was in my room, of course. Don't write "If you want to know, tell me!" Just tell me! You know I always want to know about everything that happens! I don't understand your map of CHIJ. I think it's wrong. CONGRATS to the new black-belt girl: Mei Yee!! I just found out Alisa has a black belt in taekwondo and a teaching certificate too. Her master has seven dan in black belt. No wonder she has such beautiful legs! My letters are written on few pages but they have a lot of words—all compressed. WRITE more and often!!!! And answer ALL my questions.

There is this guy named Matt who's quite good looking but I dislike his attitude. He's all smiles for Alisa whom he's interested in but never smiles at us!! Alisa has a great body and looks so beautiful. She has A LOT of guy friends in Malaysia.

Today, I ate potato chips (nearly the whole tube is gone) and Chicken In A Biskit (yum, yum). And the school canteen food is delicious. I just have an insatiable appetite for food, food, food. The hostelites here waste so much food every single night—it fills three huge dustbins!! What a terrible waste.

Unlike in Malaysia, the teachers here prepare for their lessons. For English, our teacher gave us two comics entitled *How To Be A Good Wife* and the other *How To Be A Good Husband*. So funny. The Accounts teacher once worked in the business group of a departmental store. She told us the importance of learning Accounts. We've an overhead projector (OHP) in our class. She even drew and coloured "WELCOME to Principles of Accounts" for the OHP. I keep some of my textbooks in my desk in school. (There's no afternoon session.)

Our History teacher is hilarious. We were learning about Malacca and it was so funny 'coz she kept saying, "Parameswara ran away and brought his wife along". She kept mentioning his wife. I find it funny that my classmates find Malay words like Majapahit, Parameswara and Palembang difficult to pronounce. They don't even understand their own national anthem because it's in Malay. They all sing very softly—I don't sing at all. And when they say the Singapore pledge or prayers, I don't join in either. One classmate of mine asked me if we live in trees in Malaysia, and whether we have radios!

Another classmate said to me that I speak very good English. (She probably thinks Malaysians only speak Malay.) I told her that since it's my best language, it doesn't count. (No one would say to an American that he speaks good English.)

We don't use exercise books here. We use foolscap paper and then file them up in ring binders.

Glossary
foolscap writing paper measuring 13 $\frac{1}{4}$ by 16 $\frac{1}{2}$ inches

I'm not sociable here at all. So sad. Sometimes I'm OK, sometimes I'm sad. Sometimes, living in a hostel is very fun, with funny people like Pau

Leen and others around. I don't really like Nicole (my roommate) very much, but she's very sociable and well-liked and *manja*. Nancy is very funny too but I don't know why most of them don't like her much. They say I'll realize after knowing Nancy for a longer time.

Pau Leen repaired my alarm clock but the alarm rings six hours ahead of the set time. If you set it at six o'clock, it rings at twelve o'clock; if you set it at three o'clock, it rings at nine o'clock!

Prep time is over. Sometimes I like it here 'coz the lessons in school are nice, like those you see on TV. No, not that nice, but still nice. We don't really get much homework. I spend very little time studying. Maybe 'coz it's still the beginning of the year.

I haven't done ANYTHING today. Yesterday, I read the dirty part of a very dirty book (really dirty) until 1 am, and today all I did was read it again. Although I spent so long reading it, I have only got to about 20 pages from the front 'coz I read only dirty parts again and again and searched for more. Am I disgusting or what?!

Tuesday 7 January

Dear Mei Yee
It's prep time on Tuesday now.

After school we stayed back for AEP until 5.30 pm. Mr Como and Mr Huff took us to Ang Mo Kio by MRT. Isn't the name Ang Mo Kio (White Person Bridge) funny? Jen Nee, Alisa and Nancy are in Mr Huff's group. I'm in Mr Como's where there're no Malaysians. Mr Como is nicer, but I prefer Malaysians to Singaporeans. Anyway, the group I was with was bad-mouthing Nancy about her constant singing. Nancy can sing high-pitched quite well; I don't know why people dislike it. Alisa doesn't like Singaporeans 'coz they bad-mouth people.

Mr Como looks like the typical fatherly type of American that you see on TV: big and bearded. I wonder if I would recognize him if I saw him in America.

We drew a scene we chose ourselves in a park, something like Mengkuang Dam. Mr Como took a photo of the scene each of us chose. We just drew with pencils today; maybe we'll paint it next week. AEP is organizing an art tour to Europe which costs over S$4000. And also a camp (everything paid by MOE) in Atlanta, USA, but they'll only choose one girl from CHIJ, and you have to prepare ten pictures, framed and all, and go for an interview. Everything in AEP is paid for by MOE, even drawing paper. With us joining (about nine new girls), MOE gave the AEP programme in our school a few thousand dollars.

Just now, after prep, the Sec 3s had a meeting to discuss what item to present for the ASEAN Scholars Orientation and I was very quiet. I feel so sad about being so unsociable and quiet. I feel quite out of place in school and in the hostel sometimes when everyone gets together. I feel terrible but here I am, stuck for years.

Wednesday 8 January

Dear Mei Yee
I wish I had someone I'm close to here. It's terrible to be without a close friend.

I've decided NOT to take Malay as first language. It's boring. I don't like it, I'll have to take the bus to the Language Centre to learn it, and I already have nine subjects including AEP. I'm learning about vernier calipers and whatsitsname … the micrometer screw or something, like your first chapter. I like lessons in school.

I'm so very sleepy in school 'coz everyday I wake up early and go to sleep late. I had to pull my eyes open and force myself not to fall asleep during History and Accounts. I like the Accounts teacher. She said she changed her job to become a teacher partly 'coz the people in the business world were very corrupt and would do anything for money. She said she'll teach us about shares and the stock market later in the year. This money business is very interesting, isn't it?

Betty said she was treated quite hostilely by Singaporeans when she first came. She said some Singaporeans dislike ASEAN scholars because ASEAN scholars are smart and there'll be more competition. But now her life here is better than her life in Malaysia.

Jen Nee is disorganized too. Sometimes worse than me. Sometimes she looks like Donald Duck with a cute, silly look on her face and walks a bit like Donald Duck.

I can't mix well with guys (what's new). There're only two or three that I smile to. Leo, a Sec 1 guy, always smiles at me and says, "Hi!" He's very crazy and sociable to everyone. And he always runs around instead of walking! Everyone thinks he's a sissy.
Love, Pei Yi

Thursday 9 January

Dearest Mei Yee
I'd already written a letter to be posted but I received your letter just now (five minutes ago) so I'm going to put this one in the same envelope too. No, I can't. It'll be too heavy. Forget the sentences above. OK. I received your letter today!

Remember I told you about Yoonphaik, the nice girl? Well, today she told me and Jen Nee about Christianity. She's a Christian and I can feel her faith and love for Jesus as she tells us about Him. She once practiced witchcraft! Voodoo and all those things! Unbelievable, isn't it???!!! I was damn shocked. She could read people's minds and had psychic powers and all that. She learned it from the satanic books. She said she used to feel very dark and empty but after believing in Christianity, she changed. I could see that her faith is very strong. She invited us to join her church.

She said (in answer to my question) that if there're two people, both equally good, and one is a Christian and the other isn't, the Christian will go to Heaven and the other to Hell. I can't accept that at all. Of course I didn't tell her that I didn't believe.

My horoscope this week says that I need to resolve a conflict with an old friend?! Yours says that you will find new surprises from old things! Oh ya, Yoonphaik used to live her life according to horoscopes!

It rains nearly everyday in Singapore.

OK, now (at last), to reply to your much aniticipated letter. I'm going to bring a lot of things here when I go back to BM, including your pencil-holder. I couldn't bring it the first time 'coz I had too many items to carry.

Now you know what I meant when I said I've got to tell you everything or it won't seem like it has happened. Have you found any close friends in BM? I haven't. I think I never will. Maybe I'll find good friends but never another best friend. I feel like my class in CHIJ is not really my class. OK, I'll buy books for you. Wow, I think you're great to pass black belt without practising. If I were to continue learning taekwondo, I don't think I would ever get a black belt. Are you happy about the Jackson thing? He must really like you a lot! Lucky you! So are you going to smile at Jackson the next time you see him? You're going to receive disgusting smiles every week!

Glad you've found such a good violin teacher. I still feel you should make use of your piano talents. I bet your violin playing will be very good. Actually I think you can really excel in any field you like if you work hard on it. You don't really work hard, do you? I'm also very lazy and hate to try my best.

The red ink and the blue ink in this letter are in the same pen. Depends on which way you turn it. Everyday, I keep thinking, "How nice if now I'm doing this with Mei Yee, how nice if Mei Yee's living in the same room as me ..." Ya, it's funny that things are happening to both of us now and we don't know what. You reply to one letter and I've already posted another, then you receive that letter and I receive your letter before you receive my letter. It's quite confusing. I mean, now I'm writing this letter but you might have just received the previous one and be replying to me while I'm replying to your earlier letter. Get what I mean? We're not in sync!

The Chem & Physics I'm studying now is quite easy 'coz I'm not in the Science stream. I like Accounts 'coz the teacher is nice. She decorates her transparencies (for the overhead projector) nicely and colours it, and it makes lessons interesting.

Last night after prep, there was a Batchlings (each class is a "Batch" so all the Sec 3s are my Batchlings) meeting again to plan for our Orientation. We tried to plan a sketch with a dance in it. I wasn't as quiet as in the first meeting. Anyway, we couldn't decide on anything so we chose three guys and three girls to form a committee. You could have helped give ideas and dances if you were here. Your creativity would have been useful.

I think I'll stop here and post this.

Oh ya, we have to memorize some poems for Literature. I've memorized a love poem by Shakespeare. I don't really appreciate or like poems very much.

I was also eating potato chips when I was writing this letter!

Here're a list of ECAs I'm joining: Choir Club Music (violin), Badminton (not confirmed yet), and Malay Club (don't want to but I think it's compulsory for people who take Malay as a subject.) ECA means Extra-curricular Activities, in case you didn't know. In Singapore you get points for joining ECAs. It's also important to have some important post in the ECA instead of just being a member because all this counts towards getting a scholarship for JC (Junior College) or university.

Life would be perfect here if you were here. For one thing, if you were with me, I'd probably not be so shy and unsociable. Anyway, reply soon and goodbye and see you in 22 days' time. Hope we get to spend more time together despite all your tuitions and school.

Glossary
tuition tutoring lessons

Saturday 11 January

Dearest Mei Yee
I've just posted a letter yesterday and here I am writing to you again! Actually it's now Saturday, 12.15 am and I'm still awake. I'm feeling happier than I've ever felt since coming here.

Today is Jen Nee's birthday, and yesterday after school, Alisa and I bought Jen Nee two tubes of potato chips ('coz I want to eat potato chips!). And I made her a card. People here get sabotaged on their b'day! Like all their underwear stolen (for fun) and things like that.

Oh ya, my English Teacher told me to pronounce "their" as "there", not "thiar" like we normally say in Malaysia.

OK, to get to the point of why I'm happier: I guess I've finally realized (at last) that no matter how miserable I am 'bout you not being here, you still aren't going to be here. So I'm trying to make the best out of being here.

Yesterday at school, it was quite nice—at least I mixed with some of my classmates instead of just sitting glued to my chair and talking only to my partner. My classmates are quite nice actually. It was so funny, we were learning about Malacca in History.

Singaporeans find Malay spelling difficult. The teacher asked us a question to which the correct answer was "Laksamana". Lingling spelled it "Laksaman" (a man who sells laksa! Ha! Ha! Ha! Ha! Ha!).

Glossary

laksa Malay a spicy Malay noodle dish with shredded fish

Oh ya, I wanted to tell you this but forgot—remember I told you Nicole is so sociable and everyone likes her. Well, anyway I don't like her 'coz she's selfish, boasts about boys and is bossy. I didn't know that other people (a lot of them) also dislike her, until yesterday. I was so surprised. Nicole appears really popular, you know, and I thought I was the only one to dislike her. She likes this Sec 2 guy, Wei Keong (he's a nice guy). She tells me about how well they get along, and makes it sound like Wei Keong is the one who likes her and not she who likes him. She wants me to tease her about Wei Keong liking her. And when I do, she says, "Pei Yi, ah …" in a pseudo-irritated voice. Anyway, just a few hours ago, I asked Betty what she thinks of Nicole and that's when I found out a lot of people dislike her.

I'm also happier 'coz I get along with Betty. She came to Singapore last year. She told me about how these three guys in the hostel were *perasan* that she liked them, and then they liked her back, but actually she'd just treated them like normal friends because she's from a co-ed school. Anyway, it was very interesting. She has a lot of admirers. She's friendly to everyone, including guys. I can't be sociable with guys, like she is. The three guys really liked her. Then she made it clear to the guys that she doesn't like (the bf-type-of-like) them. Now some people think she's *hiau* for leading the guys on, then jilting them.

Glossary

perasan Malay big-headed, thinking that someone likes you romantically when they might not in fact like you at all
hiau Hokkien very flirtatious (to the extent of being cheap and easy) (used for girls only)

We're going to have a class party during recess next week 'coz the first topic for Moral is Celebration. Oh dear, I'm having problems with my Maths. I'm quite bad at Maths. I have to practise more! Last night, we went to CJC hostel to get some signatures from the ASEAN scholar seniors there. Gosh, some people have about 70 signatures and I have only 34!!! If we don't get 75% of the list, we get forfeited. Have to put more effort into it. There was one guy who asked me to tell him about myself and when I said I have two cats, he wanted to know the names. He roared with laughter at "Lolo" and when I said "Bimbo" he asked me, "Do you know what Bimbo means?" He wouldn't tell, which means it was probably something dirty. At last he told, it means "prostitute"!! (That may explain why Bimbo always gets raped by the male cats in the neighbourhood! Poor Bimbo!) Then there was another guy I was so annoyed with. He told me a pack of lies about being Betty's cousin and kept asking stupid questions about her. At first he said his name was "David", then "Leland", then "Kirk". (David is his real name.)

CJC is not a very disciplined hostel. The girls and boys can go into each other's rooms without the Father (who is the director) knowing.

Oh ya, yesterday we had a Mass in school. A Father came and it was quite boring. First he praised Lord for this and that, then we sang hymns and songs (I don't mind singing), then he said some more prayers. All together, he must have said 20 prayers but when the Catholics prayed, I didn't. Actually I was feeling sleepy. I always go to sleep late at night.
I'm glad I'm getting closer to the people at my hostel, so I'm not so lonely.

Gosh this letter is really messy. It's now 1.40 am. I'm going to stop here.
Love, Pei Yi

Hi again
It's now 1.50 am and I've just finished writing in my diary. Since I'm writing to you so much everyday, I've stopped writing a lot in my diary like I used to. Oh ya, remember I told you we call RI "Retarded

Institution"? I also thought of "Rapists' Institution", and today at CJC one guy told me they have many such bad names for every school, including mine (CHIJ), and some of them are vulgar!!

Sunday 12 January

Dear Mei Yee

It's now 1.15 am on Sunday and I still haven't gone to sleep. I have so many things to tell you. Now where do I start? Yesterday morning, we woke up late. We missed breakfast so I cooked Indomee. I just put *mee* into a pot and put boiling water from the boiler and it's ready. Then Betty, Jen Nee, Alisa and Nancy gathered in my room. We told dirty jokes and ghost stories. I got really scared 'coz the ghost stories were true. I want to tell you and see what you think, if you want to hear.

Glossary
mee *Mandarin* noodles

OK, then we went to Beauty World for lunch (ate at KFC).

Betty told me RGS is moving to a new building, becoming hi-tech and is going to be privatized. They'll have lasers in the classrooms, an underground air-rifle range, cards (like ATM cards) for buying canteen food and books and for storing your personal data in. And all classrooms will be air-conned ... Very impressive.

There's this girl Elizabeth (a new scholar, Sec 3), who flirts around with boys a lot! She's the not-shy-at-all type and really flirts! She talked about dirty things to a senior guy, who then told Betty he was so disgusted he didn't want to speak to her again.

Now, something else I must tell you. I phoned my family at about 8 pm and I was alone at the phone booth, which is on the ground floor at the end of the block. After hanging up, I heard a voice out of nowhere calling "*jie*" (sister in Mandarin) twice and I got SO scared. Betty asked me to go to her room, so I went. I told her about the incident and started crying 'coz I was real scared. She told me not to worry, that it wasn't true and all that; then she played some guitar. After a while, however, I heard the voice calling "*jie*" again! I asked Betty if she heard it but she didn't. I can't tell you how afraid I was. Betty explained that if you hear someone calling your name in the middle of the night, don't answer until the fourth call, 'coz if it's a spirit, it'll go away after the third call if unanswered.

Jen Nee's now asleep on my bed. I wanted someone to sleep with me 'coz I'm scared. Sometimes we talk bad about Nicole.

So embarrassing at dinner time! For Signature Hunt, I had to go up to two tables where the guys were sitting and say, "Hello guys, I'm here to entertain you with some singing!" And I had to sing loudly. It was very embarrassing. Then, to get one more signature, I had to go back and say, "Hi, I'm back" and sing a song that went, "Tingeling ke ling-keling ... I love you ..."

Jen Nee got sabotaged—they poured water over her head.
Love, Pei Yi

Monday 13 January

Dear Mei Yee
I feel lonely in class. I'm not close to my classmates. I prefer hostel to school a lot. The CHIJ girls are not disciplined. There's this girl in my class who's quite defiant. Our Chem teacher shouted at her for rocking her chair and fined her 20 cents to be given to the class fund. After a while, she started rocking again and was scolded again. I prefer decent, *kuai-kuai* people to undisciplined, defiant people.

I wish I wasn't the only scholar in my class. Sometimes I hate it when some girls treat me like they're *boh kam muan* 'coz I'm a scholar. It's hard to explain. You see, some girls dislike scholars 'coz they think we're clever. Today, this girl was copying someone's address from my address-book and there was this number, 4881479 (I'm using any number), and the last digit wasn't so clear—could be 9 or 4, and I said, "I think it's a 9 'coz she writes her 4 this way." And she said, "Scholars will be scholars. So clever." Isn't that insulting? OK, I don't want to talk 'bout my social problems.

Glossary

boh kam muan Hokkien envious, dissatisfied with the way things are

---

I received a calculator from my family.

I slept the whole afternoon and woke up for dinner! During dinner, Sunny and I had to go to every table and announce "Hi! I'm — and —. We're the prettiest girls on earth. Whoever wants to marry us, please raise your hands!"
Love Pei Yi

Wednesday 15 January

Dear Mei Yee
It's now Wednesday and I came back from school not long ago.

I had choir practice. We auditioned to see whether we're in Soprano 1 or 2, or Alto 1 or 2. I'm in Soprano 2. The pianist has Grade 8 but her playing is terrible. Probably all she learned were exam pieces to pass the piano exams. She bangs like anything. I've watched her play Smash Hits and she can't even play semi-quarters properly. OK, enough criticizing—I'm not good either.

I've joined the swimming club 'coz I wasn't accepted into badminton. They take old members only. I pay S$15 for a course. No meetings yet.

Yesterday, my period came during PE. Thank goodness I've put a pad in my bag a few days ago.

For AEP yesterday, we did something fun. We each copied the sketch we drew last week onto a big piece of cardboard. Then we put starch on the table (the nice part is playing with the starch) and use newspapers to create a two-dimensional effect. For example, my piece looks like this:

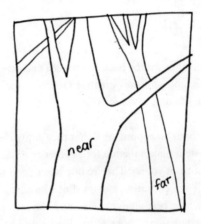

We stick layers of newspapers onto the tree trunks, so that the nearer trunks will have more layers and rise high above the paper. I was all alone during AEP 'coz Alisa, Jen Nee and Nancy are in Mr Huff's group. The girls in my AEP are sort of in cliques so I'm alone.

You know, before I came, everyone told me that it's going to be so tough studying here but it's not true at all! I'm quite free (and lazy).

There's an ASEAN scholar at my school who's staying at Marymount Hostel. There're only 36 girls there and NO GUYS! There are six girls to a room and in the whole hostel there are only four toilets! They can't go out, like go shopping! And they have nuns to watch them during prep time. My God! It sounds terrible. Their rooms have no tables, terrible!

That girl I told you about—Yoonphaik—has very funny features. Her ears are small and shaped differently from ours, and her arms have two lines at the elbows (instead of one like ours) and her arms bend like this:

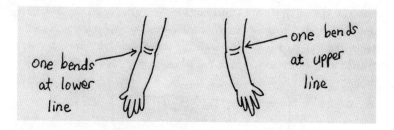

She has a line running down the back of each leg and other funny things. She told us all this, and said how creative God is to make her like this. My God, she's full of admiration for God!

A misconception about Singaporeans is that they're SO clever. Of course, their education system makes them a lot cleverer than us, but it's 'coz of the way they learn from young. They're not super geniuses or anything. What I like here is the education system. But I haven't been studying a lot or reading much or becoming cleverer and cleverer. I realized that I haven't read any wholesome books in my life before. I mean, all I read are silly kids' books, romance novels, dirty books and a lot of *Archie* comics. I'm now reading *The Barretts of Wimpole Street* which is a play the Sec 2s read last year for Literature.

Tell me 'bout everything. How's your life back in BM and at school? Are you taking tuition? Reply soon PLEASE. I'm always waiting for your letter.
Love, Pei Yi

Thursday 16 January

Dearest Mei Yee
It's late at night now. Your birthday is in half an hour's time. I've just finished rereading your old letters. When I read your letters, I giggle. This morning Nicole and I woke up so late—at 6.30 am—so I skipped breakfast. I've changed partner. Here's the sitting arrangement in my class:

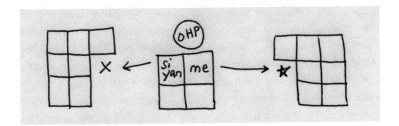

My former partner, Siyan, gave the excuse that the OHP (overhead projector) needs more space so I'm now sitting at "✶" and Siyan at "X". Siyan doesn't want to sit with me. I feel so disliked in school 'coz I have no close friends.

Swimming lessons tomorrow—I've paid S$15 for a course but I can't go 'coz period is here! Damn period. Sanitary pads here are more expensive. The only thing that's cheaper is highlighter. Only 80 cents each.

Alisa's former school in Malaysia has pupils that are rich, famous, extremely beautiful or talented. That's the impression I get but she says they're all very normal and not like what I think. One of her classmates represents Malaysia for sailing and another one of her classmates is the Sultan's grandson. Alisa is a class prefect.

She's the kind of girl that's popular and has many admirers. She eats very little and exercises a lot.

What have you been doing in BM? HAPPY BIRTHDAY! You're now SWEET SIXTEEN. Any admirers already? How's Jackson? Still so disgusting? I better go to sleep now.
Love, Pei Yi

Friday 17 January

Dearest Mei Yee
Today is your birthday. School was quite nice today. We had a class party

43

today and I took some photos. The photos are being developed at Coronation Plaza. I'm glad I'm now sitting with Huiwee and near Yoonphaik, Serena and Lingling. They're quite nice and friendly. My classmates have this stereotypical impression of me being a goody-goody, extremely clever and a bookworm. One of them was reading a trashy novel (dirty book) and when I asked her, "What book are you reading?", she replied, "You don't read this kind of book." And during some class activity, when we had to say what our favourite activity is, a girl said to me, "Reading".

Saturday 18 January

Hi Mei Yee

It's now 2.30 am, Saturday morning!! Jen Nee, Elizabeth, Pau Leen, Alisa, Nancy and I have been talking all night. Elizabeth's quite OK, I guess. I told you that everyone thinks she's a flirt 'coz she talks to all the guys. She can be quite friendly to girls when there are no guys around.

Today I borrowed a Judy Blume book, *Just as Long as We're Together*. I simply love Judy Blume!! She makes the characters in the stories SO cute and real!

I have 63 signatures now—good improvement.

For the English essay test, "Recollections of 1991", I got 27/40. Quite good. Average is 20. Most of my classmates got lower than I. Sometimes I don't feel comfortable being cleverer than them 'coz some of them don't like ASEAN scholars. I guess these are the problems many scholars face at the beginning.

God, do I love weekends!!! I hope my being quieter here than in BM ('coz you're not here) won't make me eventually a quieter person. It's 3.05 am now. Better sleep.
Love, Pei Yi

Saturday 18 January (*Later at night*)

Dear Mei Yee

Gosh! I've so (100x) many things to tell you.

Games were REALLY fun and funny today! Ha! Ha! Ha! Ha! I was in Red Team—the best team at cheating. Our leader is a spastic guy called Ekan. We played a game where we have to pass water down the line: .

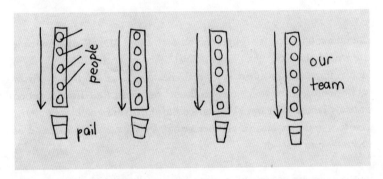

And Gaik Teong, a VERY funny guy in my Red Team, took the pail of the team next to ours and poured the water into our pail. And the other team didn't even know!!! We were all laughing like crazy. We didn't pass the water properly—we just poured it into the pail and cheated a lot. When the team next to ours poured it even slightly wrongly, Gaik Teong would shout, "Cheating! Cheating! No sportsmanship! Cheating, like little kids!" He's SO funny—I can't explain, but if you were there, you'd have died laughing!!!

The guys were all so damn funny. They caught one guy and dumped him into a mud puddle in the field. Then they caught another guy and he too got sabo (sabotaged). Nearly all the guys were dragged into the mud. So stupid and so funny! The other teams were cheering and our Red team wasn't. Then Ekan said, "Our team is special. No team spirit. No need to cheer!" So funny! Ha! Ha! Ha! Ha! They had some really nice cheers.

45

The guys were really crazy. We had to count like this:

Ekan couldn't get us to count 'coz we'd all shout "One!" and someone else would also say "One!" then "Five!" then go backwards and all. So funny. Our team members were real cheaters. Once we had to throw water bombs to see which team collected the most. Red Team collected so many before the game even started but the organizers found out and gave our water bombs to another group. Purple came in first, and us cheaters were second!

In the morning, Alisa and I went for a walk around the expensive, beautiful houses beside Hua Zhong Hostel. The designs are so unique—unlike any I've seen before in BM. I passed the house of Mr Goh something, the Prime Minister of Singapore.

Later, Betty, Jen Nee and I went to Coronation Plaza. There are two bookstores there where you can buy books and sell them back if you want (at a lower price), and they have shelves and shelves of disgusting books!!!!!!!! Imagine so many of them! I bought one.

I've got the photos already. A bit blur 'coz of my lousy camera. Cost S$9 for 35 prints. They gave a proper photo album, though, not like the lousy ones in Malaysia.

A Sec 4 girl whom most people don't like asked Jen Nee and I to do chores for her to get her signature. Like cleaning her bag and going down to take water for her. I didn't want to do that so she asked me to get a written approval from a guy saying he wants to marry me. So I asked Leo. Of course he agreed—he agrees to do anything. He's very sporting—he does everything people ask him to do to get their signatures. He looks like a pixie with sharp ears:

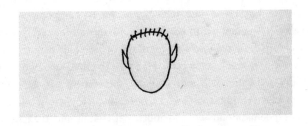

And his hair is so funny. He's from Sabah or Sarawak (can't remember which) and he reminds me of those tribes like Iban or Kadazan. Sometimes he's SO funny, and I'll laugh and laugh at his antics.

Bye, love
Pei Yi

Sunday 19 January

Dear Mei Yee
I've caught a cold.

Elizabeth and I went to buy textbooks. I bought Physics, Chem and E. Maths for you. Add. Maths is out of stock. And guess what? I bought ten CDs for only S$59!! So damn cheap—cheaper than tapes. All classical music. There are 40 volumes but I bought the first ten only. Now all I need is a hi-fi to play them on! Elizabeth said me buying CDs is like a blind man buying colour cards. But I just keep thinking how worth it it is to buy a CD for only S$5.90. We spent a few hours browsing the shops at the shopping complexes on Orchard Road. I love the humorous Valentine cards. I wonder what'll happen to you on Valentine's Day. There was a fashion show at Isetan with beautiful models. If you were there, you'd keep saying how tall and slim they were.

I made you a card this morning again!

I'm now listening to La Mer. Some of Debussy's music is scary. I've told you before but I feel like telling you again—the composers are so marvelous!! To compose music out of nothing and for every instrument, and to know how it sounds when all the instruments play together! I'm not good at recognizing pieces. Nancy recognized a Mozart piece on the radio and I didn't. Nancy is funny, sometimes, 'coz she isn't shy to sing out LOUD and then ask you, "Nice, isn't it?" or read out her essays or some poems aloud with so much expression and then say, "Nice, isn't it?"

I love weekends!! The weekdays are so long. I keep waiting for weekends and when they're here, they're gone in the blink of an eye.

Monday 20 January

Dear Mei Yee

It's now prep time. School was OK. I usually have recess with ASEAN scholars but today I had recess with Huiwee, the girl who sits beside me. One of my classmates was asking me if I had read a certain dirty book and I told her, not yet, but that sometimes I only read the dirty parts. She was surprised and said she thought she was corrupted enough but I was worse. Lingling lent me a dirty book. I've read only two chapters 'coz I spend a long time reading the dirty parts. Oh dear, why am I so yucky?! I must read dirty books less often. Alisa was saying her lips are cracking and I said, kiss more to moisten them. And she said she's bored in the afternoon so I said, "Since your window faces the boys' block, why don't you send some eye messages to them." She said she's beginning to know the kind of person I am. Ha! Ha! Ha!

Prep time over. Bye!
Love, Pei Yi

Dear Mei Yee

I reached the hostel at 6.35 pm 'coz of AEP. I'm so exhausted—last night I read a dirty book till 1 am and today I was damn sleepy in school. Mr Como said my tree artwork is nice and abstract, and he likes it. I dislike some of the girls in my AEP Club. They're always *cho kuan*. They speak so *manja* and with an accent to Mr Como 'coz he's American.

> **Glossary**
> *cho kuan* Hokkien pretentious, a pretensious person

OK. Then when I reached the hostel, I received two letters. I was SO happy. One is from you and the other from my family. I kept laughing when I read both letters. Hey, please answer my questions in my letters, OK? Wah, "the most popular girl in BM!!!!" Next time I meet you, you'll be surrounded by slaves (like Tommy). Ha! Ha! Ha! OF COURSE I'm interested in hearing all your stories!!!!!!!!!!!!!!!! Wow! Congrats! 93% for Physics!! You ARE clever. I don't know why you keep thinking I'm cleverer. When I tell Jen Nee about you (your wonderful talents in music, dancing, drawing, singing, taekwondo, the list goes on), you must have sounded like the most wonderful person God has ever created. No, I'm exaggerating. But I do admire you. Me becoming much cleverer here?! I must disillusion you on that. First I've been too lazy. I must CHANGE that!! And I haven't been learning anything that amazes me. You didn't answer my questions in my letters at all. Are you going to take Malay tuition next month? What did you get for your birthday? What did your admirers give you?

I'm coming back to Singapore after Chinese New Year by air. Sigh. So many things happening in BM and I'm not there. I wish I can be in BM and Singapore at the same time.

That's all for now and ANSWER all my questions!!!
Reply soon.
Love, Pei Yi

PS No, that's not all for now. I still have things to write. Actually being here doesn't make me very much cleverer. No, I mean of course it does. I don't know what I'm talking about. Sometimes I feel this way, sometimes I feel another way. OK. I mean being here doesn't mean I'll become as clever as you imagine, but it's nicer 'coz the school education is better, there are more opportunities, hostel life is interesting ...You know I've dreamt of hostel life since I read Enid Blyton's Malory Towers.

I even like History more now. I used to detest it so much in Forms 1, 2 and 3. People always ask why I choose 3A4 and not Science classes. I'm feeling bothered at this moment (not about being in 3A4).
Bye again, Pei Yi

Glossary

Enid Blyton one of the best-selling children books author in Commonwealth countries; she wrote over 700 books. Malory Towers is the series about girls at a boarding school.

Wednesday 22 January (*Prep time*)

Dearest Mei Yee,
I read *Just As Long As We're Together* the whole afternoon. It's such a wonderful book. You can feel what the "I" in the book is feeling. I cried while reading it. Judy Blume is a really good author! You should read that book—it's really good. And you'll see what I mean about her being so wonderful.

We did chromatography in chemistry—have you done it before? I brought back a bit of the solvent in my pen. It dissolves pen ink so I dipped my pen tips into it for fun. It made one pen write smoother. It stinks too. I rubbed it on a stamp and the stamp faded.

Alisa received a letter from a guy from CJC hostel. She won't tell who. It must be one of her admirers. A lot of people in my hostel are couples. Elizabeth looks at guys' backsides. She even said to Cheng Hoe, "You

have a cute butt."
Love, Pei Yi

Friday 24 January

Dear Mei Yee
The pens are all spoiled because of the solvent. The ink became too light.

I went swimming after school today. It was fun! I'm in the beginners'
group. Only one Form 1 girl and I can't swim so while the others learn
freestyle, we practiced floating to and fro. I've become darker—so fast.
Need to buy sunblock. I couldn't float at first, you know, but after some
time I could.

The teaching you gave me helped. Learning how to do it the second time
is much easier than the first time. The coach didn't teach me 'coz he was
teaching freestyle. I could only see blur things 'coz I couldn't wear specs.

I got S$400 scholarship money today.

The woman who collects our laundry has a wonderful memory, and I
mean wonderful. She remembers who sends what to laundry! And the
man who serves dinner onto our tray also has a remarkable memory. He
remembers who has had dinner and who hasn't.

I'm really amazed at some people's memories! Mine is simply terrible.
For example I watched the Miss America pageant and Miss Illinois
played this song and Miss Somewhere played that song and Miss Texas
wore a blue dress or something. But I'd never remember who was who
or who did what. I borrowed a book, *Memory—How to Improve It*.

At night, we played bridge. Bridge (a card game) is our hostel craze. They
even have championships! Do you know how to play? Matt explained
the game to me but I just couldn't grasp how to play it. It took me a long
time and I'm still not clear about it now. Then a warden came and

warned us not to play cards.
Love, Pei Yi

Sunday 26 January

Dear Mei Yee
We were going to watch *Doc Hollywood* with the guys but 'coz it was a nine o'clock show we wouldn't be back by the 10.30 pm curfew so one by one, we backed out. Nicole was stubborn and didn't want to back out. Anyway, in the end, Nicole, Sunny, Jen Nee and I went to Orchard Road. Elizabeth and Jen Nee talked in my room until this morning.

End of weekends. I hate school—tomorrow.
Love, Pei Yi

Monday 27 January

Dear Mei Yee
Can't wait to see you again. I was very depressed today. In the morning I felt very irritated 'coz some of the CHIJ girls are very undisciplined. They don't wear their belts or button their collars. CHIJ has a cheap reputation 'coz of some *hiau* CHIJ girls.

Why do I always go to a *hiau* school? And why do convents always have a *hiau* reputation? There's a very interesting camp called OBS (Outward Bound School) and usually very few CHIJ girls get to go 'coz of the school's reputation.
Love, Pei Yi

Tuesday 28 January

Dear Mei Yee
School was better than yesterday. I don't really enjoy AEP, though, 'coz of the people in my group. Mr Como talked a little 'bout art history and I didn't know what he was saying. During AEP, I finished first and

had nothing to do, so I did some Maths. And one of my classmates commented to me that I was so hardworking! Hardworking! Anyway, I don't want to try to change their minds anymore. They can think I'm so hardworking and I won't say, "No, I'm not. In fact …"

This is who I think is quite cute: Niles (Pau Leen's brother). I'm writing this sitting beside her and she doesn't even know.

Alisa received a love letter from Danny, a guy at CJC Hostel. At first she didn't want to tell me who it was but I kept asking and asking and at last she told. It was quite a disgusting letter. So straightforward. He even wrote "Hope we can be engaged" and "I have a crush on you".

And today there was a New Year card for her from Ekan, a guy in our hostel. Alisa is like you in some ways. The way she thinks is quite like you.

Alisa is pretty. And she has matured thinking and she's very nice too. She said that beauty is just an accident of nature and she doesn't really like being beautiful. And she's not proud that she has so many admirers. She doesn't care about having admirers.
Love, Pei Yi

Wednesday 29 January

Dearest Mei Yee
Two more days before going back to BM!!

We had a Maths test yesterday. I got OK marks. I feel that studies here are not challenging enough. Maybe 'coz I'm in 3A4. We also had an Accounts test today and two girls cheated.

The teacher was MAD. She said she HATES dishonesty. She said she's a trained teacher and can see if you cheat without walking around. She said she came into teaching 'coz in the business world everything was so evil. She could have climbed high in business but she didn't want to. And she said she now has a bad impression of our class and is going to hold back a lot of things.

Love, Pei Yi

2
Niles

Friday 31 January (*Early morning*)

Dearest Mei Yee
It's now 12.30 am, Friday 31st, the day I'm going home to BM!!!

Last night, Sunny and I watched *Police Academy* until the lights and TV
went out at 11pm, then we went back to her room. Sunny has a tiny
pocket-TV so we continued watching for a while. She told me about her
former school in PJ—so terrible. All the BGR (boy–girl relationships), all
the kissing and all the yucky things.

Sometimes, I think I've made the wrong choice coming to A4 class. It's
not competitive at all. I'd enjoy school better if I were in Jen Nee's or
Nancy's class. Anyway, it can't be changed.

I spent an hour reading dirty sections from many dirty books in Coro
today. Nancy has many, many dirty books and everyone in the hostel
(including guys) know that she reads them. Nancy and I made fun of the
way the books always describe the love-making scenes (usually the man
is very aggressive and at first unemotional, and the woman always
succumbs to his skillful love making). His searing kisses sent a shiver
down her whole body, paralyzing her with pleasure; her moan of
surrender; his mouth descended upon her swollen breasts as his skillful
fingers explored her satiny body; he looked at her naked splendor with
amazement, he kissed her fiercely, urging her lips to part ...

I bought a Judy Blume book, *Iggie's House*. Usually, Jen Nee, Alisa, Nancy and the rest will be mugging (studying) but I'll be reading storybooks or writing letters. I don't have much to study. I wish everyone hadn't said it's going to be so tough and competitive studying in Singapore. That made my dad scared I couldn't catch up so he wanted me to go to A4. The students in A4 are not good pupils, so they don't like studying and they're not competitive at all. So it's like I have no motivation to study at all.

Niles (Pau Leen's brother) is so cute.

I spent about 3 hours talking with Alisa, Nancy and Jen Nee. They asked me who's cute and I said Niles and they laughed and laughed and lost their appetite. And I told them about my crushes in BM and how I enjoyed talking to cute guys and we laughed and laughed.

Living here is fun! School isn't.
Love, Pei Yi

Friday 31 January (*At night*)

Dearest Mei Yee
This Nicole is impossible. She thinks she's so slim and beautiful. In fact she's so fat but she says she fits into all skirts. And she makes fun of Nancy's weight as if she herself is so thin. She also thinks she's God's gift to guys. She told me 'bout this guy going to talk to her. And she said she doesn't need to chase guys—they flock to her.

She kept asking me, "Do you think Wei Keong notices me? Tell me all the things that make you think Wei Keong notices me." And I would be obliged to tease her and she'd smile, pleased. Nicole is so big-headed she can't see that I'm being sarcastic. She thinks I really am teasing her.
Love, Pei Yi

Friday 7 February

Dear Mei Yee

We've been talking about child abuse and it's so disgusting! How can people EVER dig out eyes, push things up vaginas, use hammers, pliers, hot water and scissors on nipples, etc!! So sadistic!!

We did a quiz in *Teenage*—"Do people really like you?" I got 5/7 and Jen Nee and Nicole got 3/7.

Your star says this month romance is slow but it's a great time to cultivate friendships. And mine says I'll be especially attractive to the opposite sex!! So many nice articles in *Teenage*—wish you're here 'coz I want to show you. The centrefold girls are getting uglier and uglier—back to 60's style.

After dinner, Jen Nee, Nicole, Alisa and I went to Coro, where I bought some things. Nicole went on the weighing-cum-fortune-telling machine and she weighed 67 kg!! She said it's coz of her shoes! My weights was 42 kg and my fortune read: "Your pleasant manners and likeable nature win you many loyal friends." As Nicole was walking, I jokingly said, "You are walking so provocatively!" and she started to shake on purpose! When Nicole boasts and we respond sarcastically, "Wow! Wow!", she never realizes that we're being sarcastic.

At dinner, we were talking 'bout animals being tortured (eating monkeys' brains alive, cosmetics testing) and about those cruel, low-down people who torture other human beings. I got so heated-up—I really HATE those people! And then later we talked about pariahs who molest girls and I HATE them too. Once, Alisa was in a museum, and a man leaned his front on her back and she thought there must be a crowd

---

Glossary
pariah a very despicable character

behind her till she turned back. Then later, the man touched her hand. Alisa scratched him with her nails! Alisa told us that in China, they used to tie people up with nets really tight. So imagine the nets cutting into the flesh until the flesh pops out of the holes of the net. It's damn cruel. Then they slice the flesh with a knife!

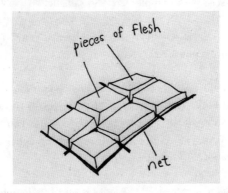

All these dreadful things happening everywhere and I can't do anything about it.

I'm going to join SPCA (Society for the Prevention of Cruelty to Animals) soon. They help to feed dogs and cats.

Niles is so cute. I seldom see him but I did see him at breakfast today. He looks very serious. And VERY CUTE! Actually, I seldom meet any of the guys or talk to them during weekdays.
Love, Pei Yi

Sunday 9 February

Dear Mei Yee
OK, about Leo, the guy you like to hear about. He likes to go to girls and touch them when he speaks to them. He is so sissy-like, my God. He shakes his hand around and he acts like a girl.

Sometimes I feel bad about being a gossip. Why do I gossip so much? I usually know people's crushes and crushees before others know.

Elizabeth mixes a lot with guys. Sometimes I feel bothered when some girls are so buddy-buddy with guys and I'm not sociable with guys. Actually, Elizabeth does treat guys only as friends but Nicole is a flirt. I saw Niles at dinner. He's SO cute. He's often alone. Betty said he is very individualistic. For example if everyone says something is nice, he won't follow them or be influenced—he doesn't follow the crowd. I like that in a guy.

Hi, I'm back from Far East Plaza in Orchard Road. I've gone shopping for three consecutive days! I spent the most. Today I bought:

1 Clip-on earnings (S$7.50)
2 A very tight tight-skirt (S$9)
3 Five blank cassette tapes, 90-minute ones (S$9.50)—blank tapes are so cheap here in Singapore

I love buying things. I saw so many nice things that I wanted to buy. If only I was rich ... It's so stupid—some things are actually very cheap, I mean, the material needed to make it is very cheap but because of the packaging and the brand, they are so expensive. The stores must earn a lot. I feel like opening some classy shops when I grow up and make lots of money! I'm going to sell expensive things 'coz the more expensive it is, the more popular it is!

All the food shops in Far East Plaza are so expensive. Jen Nee wanted to eat at one of them, but Alisa said, "Cannot, 'coz you're with Pei Yi!" and I'd eat too much and go broke. So we found a cheaper restaurant.

Leo is so terrible. When this guy chased him to snatch back a book, Leo said, "He raped me!" He asked Alisa, "Do you think Elizabeth is beautiful?" Alisa said yes. Leo whispered to me, "That depends on whether you're talking about her body or her face." Then Alisa and I (jokingly) asked Leo to leave us 'coz we don't want to be contaminated. (He was starting to touch people.)

I love listening to the radio, the classical channel. I've heard 1812, the one with cannon shots you told me about. I heard a very nice song on the radio, "Let's Talk About Sex". Have you ever heard it?

You know what?! Pau Leen knows that I say Niles is cute. (I think!) According to Alisa, Pau Leen said to her, "You know, Pei Yi ... she ... never mind ..." No wonder Pau Leen was grinning at me just now. I saw Niles again just now. SO cute!!

Singapore's nice in the sense that it's so small. So if you listen to the radio or read *Teenage*, or read the newspapers, you'll know the places they talk about.
Love, Pei Yi

Monday 10 February

Dear Mei Yee
I was so sleepy in school I fell asleep for a few seconds during chemistry but now I'm trying to sleep and can't.

The SPCA people and a very cute puppy came to give us a talk in school. The man was very funny and interesting. He said, "Don't phone us saying a cat is knocked down by a car and when we come the cat is already flat." We laughed and laughed. Then he asked some questions. Those who answered got a free SPCA calendar-postcard. Guess who got it? Yours truly (me), of course. It was so weird, people told me I'm so brave to go up and answer the questions for the SPCA.

I'm going to help out in SPCA whenever I'm free. The SPCA man said, "Everyone who goes there wants to bathe dogs but the dogs can only be bathed so many times a day. First someone bathes one, then after a while, someone else comes in and wants to bathe it."

For an English comprehension test, I got 32.5/50—highest for my class whereas in 3S3, a girl got 43/50. Oh dear, I just got Lit test today and I've forgotten the marks already. Lingling, my classmate, is treating six people, including me, to watch *Hook*, on Valentine's Day. S$7 each!! She'll spend about RM80 in total!!

Glossary
RM Ringgit Malaysia, the currency in Malaysia

Tuesday 11 February

Dearest Mei Yee
It's prep time now. I felt sleepy again in school and could hardly stay awake.

During AEP, I asked Mr Como if I could change to Mr Huff's group. I wanted to go although Mr Como is nicer, 'coz I wanted to be with Alisa and Jen Nee. He said if Mr Huff allows, then no problem. Mr Huff said he would have to see first. We drew some beach things today, then added any background we liked. I drew a rainy day background, raindrops falling on the objects. Mr Como said it was very good and later, he said he didn't want me to go to Mr Huff's group 'coz the quality of my work is very good and he said, if I really want to be with my friends, he'll let them join his group. When a Singaporean girl in Alisa's group heard about it, she said bad and untrue things about Mr Como because she didn't want Alisa to change when she herself couldn't change. She's so terrible! I really can't stand her. She tried to influence Alisa.

This morning, Niles was also at the bus stop. He takes the same bus as me sometimes. Betty said he's not cute, his face is like a stone and I said, "Have you ever seen a stone?" She said, "Yes, him" and pointed at him. Alisa's good at fast-dance. Last night, she danced in my room and she really went wild! I got very bothered about my dancing yesterday.

I cried in bed when I was listening to my Kenny G tape and thought of you. I think no one in this hostel is as terrible as me. Maybe in the whole world. I don't think they miss their best friends so much.

Today we saw a woman, thin and wearing a tight-fitting dress, walking and shaking like crazy! I've never, never in my life seen anyone shaking like that when walking. I wonder how she looks when she shakes for dancing!

Sometimes I feel I'm a terrible gossip. I'm trying to NOT bad-mouth anyone anymore. ESPECIALLY Nicole.

My classmate lent me a book full of dirty jokes. Really gross jokes—they use the "f" word and other words I've never even heard of. Another classmate lent me *Tiger Eyes* by Judy Blume. Bye!
Love, Pei Yi

Wednesday 12 February

Dear Mei Yee
I can't wait for your letter before writing to you.

I attended the Prefects' Investiture after school today. Damn boring! I wasted a whole afternoon there. So sleepy. I always resolve to go to sleep at 10 pm but end up talking until midnight or longer. Nicole, of course, enjoyed the Prefects Investiture 'coz there were some guy representatives from boys' schools. No mixing anyway—we just sat in our chairs. Some CHIJ girls were really *hiau*. They acted as if they had never seen guys. One girl who was sitting beside a guy faced away from him and acted giggly and yucky to her friends on her other side. Prefects Investiture is the ceremony where prefects get their ties and take the pledge. The Mass was most boring. I dislike Masses.

Last night, Nicole boasted (like always). She said most girls in the hostel are not sociable and are not close to Sec 4 guys, hinting that she herself is close. So I said, "Who are you close to?" and she said, "Why should I tell you?" Then she went on, "Sigh. I don't know why, every time Leo has a problem, he'll come and talk to me about it ..." I dislike, no, hate it, when people boast about something which is not true (in her case, being popular with guys) and act like they're not boasting.

Today she acted like she had a date for Valentine's Day but might not want to go. When I asked, "Who?" she replied, "Why should I tell you?"—the phrase she uses when she has no answer. And she was saying how much she hates RI guys and how spastic and yucky RI guys were to her friends during Prefects' Investiture.

I'm calling Niles "River". River flowed behind me when I was lining up and getting food for dinner.

Alisa said she doesn't like it when people say she's beautiful 'coz A) It creates a gulf between her and others; B) People praise her in front of her younger sister and she feels "not nice"; C) People might like her for her beauty only.

You know, people treat you nicer if you're pretty. If you're pretty, a lot of people will want to befriend you 'coz they like to be seen with beautiful people. Many people in my school like to mix with Alisa. Well, maybe it's not 'coz of her beauty only 'coz she does has a very nice and friendly personality.

I hope you come for JC (Junior College). If I know that you're coming, I will feel happy coz I'll have something to wait for and the days will go faster.

I'm wondering, if a bird hovers in the bus and the bus moves, will the bird knock the back of the bus? Or if we jump up in a moving train, will we land back in the same spot? Pau Leen just saw me writing the letter and she said, "Again!?" If only she knew I had been writing about her brother!
Love, Pei Yi

Thursday 13ʰ January

Dear Mei Yee

I know I should be doing something more constructive now but I have so many things to tell you.

OK. Ekan asked Alisa out for Val Day last night and she didn't want to go but she said, "I'll think about it." Just now she went to him and said she's busy and can't go and she asked me to call her so that she wouldn't have to stand there with him so I did. Alisa received three Val Day cards today. Two from a guy she met at Club Med during Chinese New Year hols. The guy is in love with her. One of the cards reads something like, "I don't know you well but I know you're everything that I want and need and I know I'm in love with you." Alisa was bothered 'coz the guys she's friendly towards always fall in love with her whereas she just treats them as normal friends. So you either get called cheap or snob. She wrote a letter explaining to him that she doesn't feel the same way towards him. Alisa receives so many letters everyday! And nearly all the guys compliment her on her looks. She doesn't like it if we say something about her always getting compliments, though.

Did I tell you, yesterday, Nicole told everyone she's going out with her date on Val Day and she said, "I'm so excited …" but we just found out that the guy Nicole's been boasting about is just a family friend whom her uncle had asked her to meet.

Last night, Alisa, Nancy, Jen Nee and I talked until 12.30 am. I MUST sleep early tonight!! Mr Huff won't let Jen Nee and Alisa come to my group!!! He's so mean. Alisa told him, "If we don't go to Mr Como's group, Pei Yi is going to be miserable" and he said, "Well then she'll have to be miserable for two years!"!! Betty told me, there was a girl who wanted to quit AEP so she told Mr Huff and he said, "You want to go? OK! BYE!" as if he didn't care at all. (He didn't.)
Love, Pei Yi

Friday 14 February (*Valentine's Day!!*)

I wonder what happened to you today. Who did you receive Valentine cards from? Alisa received a V card from Ekan and one with unknown initials.

I was waiting for school to be over the whole day.

Nicole came back from her date—which wasn't a date—so happy. Sunny, who used to say that Nicole's OK and that I was prejudiced against her, said today she has changed her mind. She hates Nicole too now—Nicole boasted to her about her date giving her three yellow roses (maybe she bought them herself) and hundreds of other things.

I don't think you understand how much I wish you were here. Maybe no one does. Maybe God wants me to learn to do without you. Well, reply SOON. I haven't received any letter from anyone since Chinese New Year.

This is one of the times when I feel miserable and I'm listening to Kenny G. The track "Silhouette" is very nice.
Love, Pei Yi

Saturday 15 February

Dearest Mei Yee
I woke up in the morning with a headache at ten o'clock. Then Alisa and I went to Orchard Road, where I bought a book, *The Fine Art of Flirting*. I'm keeping it a secret 'coz if I don't, it'll be embarrassing. I haven't read it yet. I wrapped the cover with paper from a large calendar so that no one will know what I'm reading.

I read *Tiger Eyes* by Judy Blume. It's very sad 'coz it's about a girl dealing with her father's death. I cried.

I saw River at dinner. So cute. Since knowing how individualistic he is, I don't always follow the crowd anymore. For example, if everyone gets together to talk, I would've felt bothered in the past if I was excluded. Not exactly bothered, but I'd feel I should join them and not miss anything. But now, I feel more comfortable doing what I like. Sometimes I really enjoy being alone.

I like Singapore, you know. I've always liked living in an advanced, clean place, living in a hostel, going out when I like. It's very easy to go out here and travel anywhere.
Love, Pei Yi

Sunday 16 February

Dearest Mei Yee
Just now, I watched a show about the Japanese Occupation. The old people told of how they were tortured last time. It's so cruel and disgusting!! I was so horrified I nearly cried. Betty said some pregnant female spies who were not supposed to get pregnant, were tied by one leg to a tree. Then three buckets of water were tied to one leg and the hands, and the body was split up at the vagina and the womb fell out! There were many other inhumane stories. I don't understand how the soldiers could have had the heart to do those things.

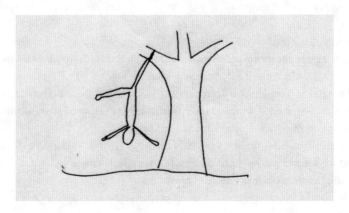

Sometimes Alisa is quite cold to me. I don't know why and I don't care. For lunch, six of us together with six guys went to KFC at Beauty World. I bought something AGAIN! I must stop spending so much. I bought a white sleeveless blouse. I love the soft silky material. It has a sash to tie at the hips or you can tuck it in and has buttons running down the front. It cost S$20. I also bought a book, *Girl Talk*, for S$6.90.

Val Day is VD which is Venereal Disease!

Alisa said to me during prep, "Pei Yi, sitting beside River's sister" and Pau Leen was just sitting beside me! I've decided not to trust so many people anymore and to keep my secrets to myself. I nearly wanted to tell Sunny and Jen Nee about the flirting book but didn't. I'm not telling my secrets anymore to so many people.

Our Chemistry teacher pronounces her Rs so clearly I giggle every time she speaks. "Good morning, girrrrrls."
Love, Pei Yi

Wednesday 4 March

Dear Mei Yee
It's not my turn to reply but I just want to talk to you. I came back from St John's Island Camp today. It was quite OK. But I would've enjoyed it a lot more if A) I didn't have my period (what luck to have period during camp!); B) Didn't have headache; C) Didn't have cough and running nose (skipped jogging and exercise because of that); D) You were there.

I missed the hostel and you when I was there. I made many new friends though. I learned how to pitch a tent and cut my finger in the process.

I received a letter from my sister that made me so sad. Yi Hoon said that she misses me. And even when I go back, she still misses me 'coz I'll be spending all my time with you. She said I only stay at home during meal-times and bedtime. She said I'm like Bimbo (the cat), staying for food only. And she said she's jealous when I talk more to you. I cried when I was reading it. I feel so bad. My whole life is in a mess. Why didn't you apply for the scholarship!? If you were here, I wouldn't be miserable and I'd be able to spend more time with my family when I go back.

It's prep time but I skipped it 'coz of headache. I have been wasting time the whole night. I read a really good book, *The Dream Collector*. It's about a girl buying a book that teaches her how to make her wish come true. Her wish was to get John to like her but when he did, she'd liked Tom instead. I wish my wishes would come true. Jen Nee said sometimes I'm so happy and sometimes so miserable—extreme mood swings— whereas Jen Nee seems to always be quite happy. I've never seen her sad. I think the trick is to be occupied. I'm going to write to Yi Hoon now. Bye.
Love, Pei Yi

Thursday 5 March

Hi Mei Yee
I feel so lonely. Have you ever felt like you don't feel like mixing with anyone? I'm in school now. Earlier, when I got on the bus, River also got on. He went up to the upper deck though. He's SO cute. I'm so sad that there's nothing that can happen between us. Why is it that the guy I like never likes me back?
Love, Pei Yi

Dear Mei Yee
Hi! Just now I had lunch with Serena, my classmate. She's SO crazy and funny. Now she looks like a poodle 'coz she permed her hair wrongly.

We ate KFC and laughed and laughed. A few of my Singaporean classmates thought that I'm Malay and that I'm a Muslim! Ha! Ha! Ha! Once, Serena laughed till her jaw was dislocated! She had to go to the hospital.

Sunny told me she had a friend who keeps accounts of all her expenditures! She opens account journals for every single cent spent, and if she finds a few cents gone, she opens *akaun tergantung* (pending account). So funny!

Teens mag chooses four girls every month to give them makeovers and see how beautiful they become. Honestly, the girls became uglier. Anyway I entered the contest. Sent two photos of myself. I do have a bookworm look, don't I? Many of my classmates think so. That's why they think I'm studious and all.
Love, Pei Yi

Monday 9 March

Dear Mei Yee
Guess what happened during dinner?! I talked to River!!! Can you believe it? I hardly believe it myself. Unfortunately it was just the one sentence.

Let me tell you about it from the beginning. Sunny and I and a few others were having dinner and Sunny asked me to take more soup for her. I said, "No." Then Sunny said River is in the queue, waiting in line with his tray. So she said, "Go go go!" I waited for River to go nearer to the soup pot, then I walked over and took some soup. I turned to River and said, "Were you late for school this morning?" He looked a bit surprised then smiled and said, "Ya." I wanted to say that Jen Nee and I were also late but I was so nervous that I couldn't. Instead I giggled, sort of half-giggled half-laughed! Can you imagine!? How stupid of me. I just couldn't control myself. Anyway, when I walked back to the table, Jen Nee and Sunny were laughing and laughing. They had heard something like, "Why are you so late?" but I didn't tell them what I really asked. I sounded nervous and shaky when I asked him; I hope he didn't notice. Anyway, that's all there is to tell about this important event.

Today was a BAD day. First, Jen Nee and I were late to school 'coz we missed the bus by one minute. River also missed it. After a long wait—I didn't mind 'coz River was also waiting—the bus came. So many people were going up and a second bus came so we took the second one but River took the first one. We were booked for being late. I'm going to have to do detention class soon.

School was miserable. I don't have close friends in my class. Maybe I shouldn't look so miserable in class. And I know Elaine and Lingling, who sit near me, are bad-mouthing me. I know 'coz when I went near them, Elaine realized I was near but Lingling didn't and Elaine sort of pointed at me, and they stopped talking and looked like they'd just talked bad 'bout me. I don't know why I feel so bothered 'coz of two girls. I realized that I like my classmates better than Jen Nee's classmates. Some of the girls stick to Alisa. They're that kind that stick to pretty girls.

Bye!
Love, Pei Yi

3
Chicken Pox!

Sunday 22 March

Dearest Mei Yee
Jen Nee and I are back in Singapore now! Jen Nee's got chicken pox.
She's staying in her room for two weeks and missing school.

I saw River (Niles) in the hostel field today; he was topless. He has a
nice, firm body. Sunny made up all these stupid stories about River, and
I laughed.

Today, I read Christopher Pike's *See You Later*. A very (10x) good book!
Full of suspense and mystery. Quite a sad ending, though. I'm feeling sort
of depressed and empty. I think something must be wrong with me to feel
depressed so often.

No news about the makeover. Maybe they won't choose me at all. I'm
just feeling depressed now. Wish Jen Nee didn't have chicken pox! She
can't do anything with me now! Got to sleep, it's past midnight. I wish
for the millionth time since coming here that you were here.
Love, Pei Yi

Monday 23 March

Dear Mei Yee
So much work to do!

Sunny and Jen Nee asked Pau Leen if she knows that I like her brother. She replied, "Aiyah …!" which means, "Who doesn't know?" I shouldn't have told people. It all started with me saying he's cute—I didn't even like him then—which is nothing wrong, then I started to like him. They asked Pau Leen if Niles knows about it, and she kept saying, "What do you think?" as usual. Then she said Niles doesn't know. (Phew!) I think I've given up hope chasing guys. Maybe I will end up being single. When you imagine your future, do you always see yourself as a married woman? I do. Hope I do get married.

Love, Pei Yi

Dear Mei Yee

Guess what? I entered 200m swimming heats today. And not only came in last but was SO far behind everyone else!

I feel so desperate about River. I didn't smile at him even when I saw him at the bus stop. It's 'coz he always looks so fierce and unapproachable. But maybe he only looks unfriendly 'coz he doesn't want to be the kind of person who's always smiling. I wish I'd smiled at him!! I should have!! We got on the same bus. I went up to the top deck and later he came up, and sat in the empty seat in front of me. I could have talked to him BUT didn't!! My heart was beating so hard and fast! (Nancy would have called it "thumping against the walls of my chest".) I was debating with myself whether to talk to him when my bus stop came into sight. My first step is to smile at him. I MUST when I next see him.

Did I tell you about this: Alisa and Pau Leen were watching the Sec 3 and 4 guys play basketball. River was also playing. Alisa told me Pau Leen said, "Pei Yi should be here."

Love, Pei Yi

Tuesday 24 March

Dearest Mei Yee

Guess WHAT!? I checked the messages today and found out that Penny

Kim of *Teens* had called me on 16/3. I called her back but she had already gone home. I think it's about Makeover of the Month. Hope (really hope) that I can be on 'coz she called eight days ago! Maybe she just called to say, "Sorry but your face is too bad, we can't fix it." I checked the mag and saw that she's the stylist and coordinator. I'm now writing with thumb and middle finger 'coz my index finger's hurting. You should've seen me—I was SO excited 'bout being chosen! I told Sunny, "The Beginning of the Life of a Supermodel." She joked, "What are you going to model? Dwarf's clothes?" Can't wait to hear the news!

I was so sleepy during AEP. Mr Como was explaining art history and he said, "Don't fall asleep on me." I felt so bad. Then we drew three sweets. Mine was yucks.

Tomorrow is my Lit test and I'm not even reading! I got back at 5.45 pm after AEP.

Then spent my time being excited over *Teens*. Then dinner and prep (read *Teenage* and wrote letters).

I wonder if we'll ever be studying or staying together in the future. After school and university we'll be working and getting married and living separate lives. I wonder if we'll live in the same town. Will I continue writing letters to you all my life?

Sigh, sigh, sigh, sigh, sigh. Good night.
Love, Pei Yi

Dear Mei Yee
You'll never believe my BAD luck. I WAS chosen for Makeover of the Month but Penny Kim said it's over—during hols. I begged her to put me in for the next month, but she said she couldn't 'coz it wouldn't be fair to the new entrants. I'm so sad and disappointed. I even cried in school. No one understands how much I wanted this and how sad I am. Oh Mei Yee, why, why, why???? I can still send in more entries, of course. But I

might not be chosen anymore!

About the lift, you said if the cable breaks and the lift falls, the person inside will crash through the roof? I don't think so 'coz the person will also be accelerating at $10m/s^2$, right? Today we learnt that if the cable breaks, a person standing on a weighing scale in the lift will be weightless. I don't understand why 'coz the lift and the person are accelerating at the same rate.

Love, Pei Yi

Wednesday 1 April (*April FOOL'S Day!*)

Dearest Mei Yee

Jen Nee and I went for a medical checkup today. I had to undress completely except for my panties and lie on the bed while the female doctor touched me all over. I laughed and giggled (ticklish) and the doctor was quite grim. She didn't say anything about breast cancer BUT she said I have heart trouble! I have to go for another checkup on 2 May! I was so depressed. I mean, you hear of people getting heart attacks, being raped, getting AIDS etc, but you don't ever think it'll happen to you. Don't tell anyone about this. I only told Jen Nee and Sunny. I'm afraid that something is seriously wrong with me. What if they say I'm going to die soon!? I must stop indulging in self-pity.

Remember I told you about two girls in my class who were bad-mouthing me? Well, actually they weren't. I found out today that I was a jerk. Huiwee, Elaine, Lingling and Serena were actually planning my birthday present, which they gave me today.

I feel like such a terrible JERK. Sometimes I'm really a horrible person. They gave me a letter pad (it's obvious that I always write letters), a lucky troll (very cute) and a compact stationery set. All from Art Box, a very expensive gift shop, the kind I'd like to open next time. They must have spent A LOT on the jerk, yours truly.

Here's a list of my birthday presents:

> Nancy—a cute small photo frame, a card
> Alisa—potato chips
> Betty—poster (that cute kind with a little girl in pastel colours)
> Classmates—cards and chocolates
> Jen Nee—will give one after her chicken pox
> Sunny—a book called *Coping with Periods*

I received your letter today. Wow, you and Jay! If Molly knows she'll kill you! But, who cares 'bout her? Do you like him? Are you happy 'bout it or what? Do you mean Jay spoke to you for two hours or *The Magic Flute* was two hours?

My letters aren't short! Have you received the long one? Hey, please answer my questions in my letter, OK? Well, maybe my letters are shorter 'coz I write them in a day instead of continue every day like I used to. What am I going to do about my heart?! I feel so sad 'bout it. I don't feel like writing now.
Love, Pei Yi

PS Would you feel awkward being naked in front of doctors? It's a terrible experience that I'll probably have to undergo once more on 2 May. Oh dear, I hope it's nothing too serious like "You have six years to live!"

Venue: Prep room
Time: No watch, but I think it's 8.15 pm
Date: April
Age: 16 already! How fast!
Feeling: Depressed but pretend not to be

Glad I received your long-awaited letter
Love, Pei Yi

Saturday 4 April

Dear Mei Yee

Guess what? I have chicken pox! I'll have about two weeks of no school, excess porridge and lots of time to write to you. Gosh, it's so difficult to write with my left hand. I found a spot on my palm and one on my leg (isn't it weird, you'll probably imagine them at the wrong places on the palm and leg) this morning. Last night I had a fever.

Am staying here, despite protests from some hostelites. Jen Nee is quite displeased about some people blaming her for spreading chicken pox to me and another girl.

This morning, Jen Nee and I went to Toa Payoh to see the doctor but first we walked around the shops. I bought ten blank tapes for S$18 and a 2nd Chance shirt for my dad for S$26.90 using my S$10 voucher. Had lunch then went to the clinic but it was closed (half day today) so I had to go to a private doctor. It cost Jen Nee S$36 when she consulted that doctor but I paid only S$17 'coz I could get most of the medicine from Jen Nee (unfinished). The doctor said I can eat anything except deep-fried food. When I told him my friends said I shouldn't eat cucumber, prawn, black sauce, chicken and so forth, he said it's just superstition.

Tomorrow, all the Sec 3s in my hostel are going to Sentosa Island but I can't. Oh dear, I don't want to miss school. I can't stand missing the fun. Last night, Sunny, Jen Nee and I walked around the housing estate and talked in the dark about the gross and cruel things that happen in Asia (eg, the lives of prostitutes).

Sunny also likes to bad-mouth people. Because she's a confident and interesting person, and also good at storytelling, usually we like to listen to her talking and complaining about others, eg Nicole, Alisa and several others. And I know that deep down, I also like to listen to her bad-mouthing people because it makes me feel like I'm slightly better than those people, but it's actually bad to be like this; I wouldn't be

enjoying this gossip if I were a more confident person myself. I asked Jen Nee what she thought about all of this. She said someone told her that the bible says gossiping is bad. I was surprised that the bible actually talks about such ordinary things like gossiping! Jen Nee and I decided that the next time Sunny talks bad about someone, we should just try to change the subject and not participate even if it's tempting.
Love, Pei Yi

Sunday 5 April (*2 pm*)

Dearest Mei Yee
Everyone is at Sentosa Island. I'm in my room.

I found an old copy of *Teens* in someone's wastepaper basket so I took it. What do you think of being a cover girl? I think they're very lucky.

My chicken pox has become worse. Yucks (10x)! It makes my body look like a toad—disgusting!! I hate chicken pox!!! My whole body is full of yucky spots. They itch and hurt a bit when touched. Scratch, scratch, scratch. Can't imagine how Jen Nee could be so happy when she was having chicken pox.

I've plenty of time so I'm reading *Teens*, Christopher Pike's *Final Friends I*, and *The Fine Art of Flirting*.

My chicken pox is so yucky, itchy and uncomfortable! It's 8.10 pm and I'm feeling lonely and miserable.
Love, Pei Yi

Monday 6 April (*Hari Raya hol—only a day!*)

Dearest Mei Yee
My chicken pox has become even WORSE! My God, I'm so horrified with myself. I can't stand this kind of thing and now it's spreading all over me!

My dad is here. He left BM last night and reached Singapore in the morning.

I was so itchy yesterday. At night I was afraid that I'll see ghosts 'coz you told me that we can see them if we're sick. So I didn't dare to open my eyes. My stupid chicken pox is really very severe! I hope tomorrow it doesn't get worse! Oh please God, help me now, I'm suffering!

Cried 'coz I was afraid my chicken pox would get worse and worse till none of my skin can be seen anymore.
Love, Pei Yi

Glossary
Hari Raya *Malay* the day celebrated by Muslims signifying the end of the fasting month of Ramadan. The celebration is determined by the sighting of the new moon.

Wednesday 8 April (*6.30 pm*)

Dearest Mei Yee
Hi! Wow it's been four months since I first came to Singapore! It doesn't seem that long. I used to cry and cry during the first month! I hardly cry now. The last time I cried was when I found out 'bout the makeover and a few days ago when I was so afraid the chicken pox would keep spreading until I have no skin left visible.

Well, my chicken pox is still bad but not that itchy anymore. I think I'm going to have a lot of scars on my back. I estimate there are 800 spots on my body. No, maybe 500.

Usually, people who get chicken pox in my hostel will go back but this year, Jen Nee and I didn't. Jen Nee said that Sunny said that Alisa said that Jen Nee and I are inconsiderate 'coz we stayed here with chicken pox. They can hate me, I don't care. I'm fed up with hearing "They shouldn't stay here", "They will spread it to everyone", "Why don't they go back?"!

I feel very grateful to Jen Nee and Sunny for caring for and helping me while I had chicken pox. Especially Jen Nee. Why is she such a nice girl? Jen Nee was enjoying herself reading and lazing around when she was ill. I couldn't enjoy myself 'coz I felt quite sick, but now I feel quite OK. I hope I'll fully recover soon. My case is a lot worse than Jen Nee's. I thought of phoning you tonight but I can't leave my room.

I've read *The Prom Queen*, *Falling Into Darkness* and I'm now reading *Final Friends II* by Christopher Pike. He's a very good author!

I'm missing school and what is being taught. I like Maths period best. What about you? I dislike PE. I like Malay period too, not 'coz of the teacher but 'coz I sit with Jen Nee.

These few days, I haven't been doing much 'coz I wasn't feeling too good. I heard a lot of nice songs on the radio though. I listened to "I Love Your Smile". Actually I heard it sometime ago but I didn't know it was that song. I like these songs (I'm not really sure 'bout the titles), do tell me whether you like them, if you know them:

1 "Crying"
2 "I'll Be There"
3 "If You Go Away"
4 "Heal the World" (Michael Jackson)
5 "Beauty and the Beast" (Celine Dion and Peabo Bryson)
6 "What Becomes of a Broken Heart"
7 "Masterpiece"
8 "The First Time"
9 "Heaven"
10 "Heal the Pain"
11 "When You Tell Me That You Love Me" (Diana Ross)

Anyway, I no longer like Niles.

The guys who are quite nice are: Cheng Hoe, Matt. The others I seldom talk to but they're also nice. Actually I hardly talk to guys.

It's now 7.10 pm. Jen Nee just brought my porridge. Tasteless porridge— yucks. So unappetizing. Luckily Sunny bought chicken rice for me for lunch and Jen Nee bought me a ham roll. I think I better eat my porridge now.

Waiting for your letter.
Love, Pei Yi

Thursday 9 April

Dear Mei Yee
My dad came this morning. He went back in the afternoon. He really cares so much for me. I miss family life. Especially after being in this room for seven (?) days.

Physics is driving me crazy. I missed the lesson on action–reaction (Newton's Third Law) so I read it myself. I don't really understand it. I mean, if you push a block of wood and the wood pushes back (equal reaction) why would it move? If everything has a reaction force how can anything move anything. My mid-year exam is in May. My mind has gone rusty this week—I haven't done anything except read storybooks. I can't bear missing lessons being taught in school!!

Being cooped up in my room for so many days makes me lonely and sad. I sort of miss life in BM. Sometimes I feel so alone in this world. Have you ever felt that? You know, you're lucky to live with your family. At times like this (when I'm feeling alone) I miss them. Sometimes I wonder what life is all about. Going to school, trying to excel, study, study, study, study, graduate, have a career, get married, have children, grow old, die.

My plans when I recover:

1 Be more awake in the morning—sleep at the right time
2 Utilize time—study hard and read books
3 Borrow and read books from the library
4 Exercise and diet well
5 Socialize, be a nicer person

Friday 10 April

Dearest Mei Yee
I just got up and it's 12.20pm! I slept late (2.30 am) reading *Final Friends III*, the last in the series. I read the romantic parts again and again. They're not dirty at all, but they seem so sweet, so romantic, and I feel so touched. Just now, I dreamt that I was home and Niles phoned and said he and a few others were coming to my house to watch a video. Then he stayed longer than the others. A nice dream. I also dreamt, Niles told me he used to have a crush on Brad!! And I said, "Me too!"

And I couldn't wait to tell you 'bout him and me, but it turned out to be a dream. I WANT Niles. I don't know why I never get over him.

You know, the guys in Christopher P's books make me think of Niles. After reading his books, I'll think of him. Now I'm craving for a guy-friend but I'm stuck in my room. I feel so bored.
Love, Pei Yi

Saturday 11 April

Dear Mei Yee
I'm feeling very lonely and sad. I wish you're here 'coz then I wouldn't be bored or lonely. I'm afraid of loneliness. I mean, what if I grow up, don't know many people, don't get married and end up very lonely? I wish I'd gone home when I first had chicken pox. At least I would have had my family close by and I could have gone for walks or something—

anything would be better than being in a room. My social life is now ZERO. I'm totally bored with my life. God, what is happening to me?

I'm now reading a horror book, *The Bad Place*. Don't understand what they're saying. Can't stand it—why do they have to write it so hard and complicated when an easy way can be used? What books have you read recently?

How's your life? What have you been doing, what's been happening? Bet it's not half as boring as mine. Can't stand it—I didn't receive a single letter since last week or maybe longer still. Hate eating porridge.
Love, Pei Yi

Dear Mei Yee
Hi! Jen Nee has two things in common with you—her pens can't write and she slips all these pieces of paper between books.

Yesterday I broke my biggest chicken pox on my leg accidentally! I think I'm going to be scarred a lot!

Your letter was very funny. My God! Your uncle is SO rich! I can't stand it. S$1000 for a pair of ugly red swimming trunks!? S$230 for breakfast?! Are the hotel people crazy? How can you stand it? It strikes me as very terrible that there're people suffering somewhere in the world but not far away, there're people spending money like it's nothing! You're SO lucky to stay in Mutiara Hotel! I feel sorry for your uncle too. He's so kind and generous. Aargh! I can't stand money being wasted on women and gambling. And I can't stand it when people are taken advantage of 'coz of their generosity.

My God, why do you keep feeling inferior?! I think you're very lucky 'coz everywhere you go, people, I mean guys, will look at you or want to know you.

While you were enjoying yourself in Mutiara, I was suffering here with chicken pox!

I've finished *The Bad Place*. It turned out to be REALLY great. I really admire the author. He can really make me feel when I read it. For example when he was describing Thomas, the poor man with Down Syndrome, I felt the way Thomas thinks is so cute and he's so pitiful. This is the first thick novel I've read.

Well, hope to hear from you soon! Ciao!
Love, Pei Yi

Thursday 16 April

Dear Mei Yee
Hi! I've just posted a letter to you but here I am, writing another one! I feel like I'm talking to you when I'm writing—that's why I like to write. Yesterday, I came out of my room for the first time since chicken pox to play badminton outside Block A. I love badminton. I played again this morning.

Why is it, I wonder, that girls are called *hiau* and cheap but if guys fool around, they're considered, "wow, playboy, conquer so many ..." and never *hiau*. You know we used to call PFS (Penang Free School) "Panties For Sale"? Well, Jen Nee calls it "Penang's Faggot School" (faggots are homosexuals).
Love, Pei Yi

Sunday 19 April

Hi Mei Yee!
I'm so happy to be well again! I went to McD for lunch with Jen Nee and Sunny. Cheeseburgers only 88c.

You know, since coming here, I've become different in the sense that now I care 'bout my studies. Last time I didn't care about exam marks. Now

I do, a lot. And Jen Nee is like the old me—she doesn't study. She's always wasting her time. But she still does well in school. She only studies when there're tests. I keep feeling pressured to be clever. The environment here is nice for studying.

Love, Pei Yi

Monday 20 April

Dear Mei Yee

Hi! I'm so happy to go back to school. But I've got a lot of catching up to do. Mrs Simons is so kind! I told her I don't understand Maths 'coz I missed that chapter so she said she'll teach me when I stay back on Friday.

After school, Jen Nee and I went to Toa Payoh Library then ate McD. We read about Van Gogh and admired the beautiful, wonderful paintings.

Lingling wants to give me tea because I'm supposed to wash away my chicken pox poison. Another of my classmates got chicken pox: Elaine. One after another!!

I asked Alisa if she has started studying for mid-year exams and she said no but her roommate said she started last month. So I guess she pretends to be lazy so that we'll be too. So Jen Nee and I have decided to study intensively and pretend that we're not.

Love, Pei Yi

Wednesday 22 April

Dear Mei Yee

I should be doing my work and studying now but I want to talk to you.

Tomorrow is the Swimming Carnival so we're going to Toa Payoh Swimming Pool in the afternoon. Don't have to sleep so early—it's now

1.20 am and Jen Nee's in my room. She's always reading Physics or Chem while I'm reading History or Lit. Lit is interesting. We're doing a bit of *Merchant of Venice* now. It's nice 'coz when I first read it, I don't understand it AT ALL but after the teacher explains, I do understand it. BUT during the exam, I'm dead. Mid year!!! 4 May!!! I know yours is over.

Jen Nee got a conduct form for making noise after 11 pm. The assistant manager, whom everyone HATES, has something against her, and tries to catch Jen Nee at every opportunity! She even accused her of talking when she wasn't. I also had to fill out a form explaining why I was talking after 11 pm but I didn't get a conduct form. After three conduct forms, we have to do some hostel chore in public, like picking up all the rubbish in the field.

In Jen Nee's class, there are some girls who're VERY good in English. There's this girl, Germaine, who's not only good in English, but also VERY rich and proud. You know, that kind of Engish-speaking-brought-up-in-an-English-like-family-and-shows-off-big-words girl.

PS Just remembered, Jen Nee told me that a girl asked Alisa whether she has studied Art History and Alisa said she hasn't even TOUCHED it but actually Jen Nee has seen her bringing Art History books to prep twice. Oh dear, EXAMS, EXAMS, EXAMS!!! Every time a big exam comes and I'm supposed to be studying I'll have a craving to do something like read storybooks. I don't like appearing studious to ASEAN scholars but I don't mind appearing studious to my classmates. Sigh.

Better say bye.
Love, Pei Yi

Dear Mei Yee
Hi! I received your letter when I came back from the Swimming Carnival. We all received a certificate for going to the Carnival—it's part of the Singapore culture to collect as many certificates as possible. It's

now prep time and I'm sleepy.

These are things I was supposed to do today:

1 Prepare Van Gogh essay and study 'bout Impressionism
2 Prepare many, many History essays
3 Prepare Lit essays, memorize poems
4 Paint sweets for AEP but I've lost my sweets
5 Do Physics homework
6 STUDY

This is what I actually did:

1 Woke up at 8.30 am, read newspapers
2 Went to Coronation and bought S$30 worth of food and developed photos
3 Jen Nee had Chem extra class today but she overslept so we spent 40 minutes assembling a sweetshop cut out from the back of a box of Koko Crunch
4 Went to eat chicken rice for lunch
5 Walked around Crown Centre. I was looking for a nice birthday card for Betty but couldn't find one special enough. Bought a green one-piece dress at a shop that was having sales—all clothes only S$10 each. Actually it was for Betty's birthday but I like it so much I've decided to keep it for myself.
6 Jen Nee and I went to the Swimming Carnival—we were late and got booked. This is the third time I've been booked! I'll be going to Detention Class soon.

At the Swimming Carnival, I sat beside Alisa and found out that she's very pretentious. Jen Nee realized it too. It's very hard to explain. For example, at Swimming Carnival or Sports Day, she pretends to be so enthusiastic and spirited and loyal to our house and she cheers and cheers. No, that's not it. But she's just very pretentious. I can't explain it!! It's her tactic to become popular. Sometimes I understand what

people are trying to do even if they don't tell me.
Love, Pei Yi

Sunday 26 April (*Morning*)

Dear Mei Yee
Hi. It's now 12.30 am on Sunday. Yesterday we were at the library reading about Van Gogh from morning to 4 pm. When we came back from the library, Alisa asked us where we'd been. Then she said we're so hardworking, blah, blah, blah. Aargh. I feel so *geram* 'coz I've tons to tell you but there's too much to write and I have to do my work.
Love, Pei Yi

Glossary
geram Malay irritated, bothered by something

Monday 27 April

Last night, Jen Nee and I fee asleep on my bed at 3.40 am. I woke up at noon and watched *Growing Pains* and *Beverly Hills 90210*. What shows do you watch now?

Nancy lent me a copy of *All Stars* mag. They used to have *NKOTB* in every issue; now it's *Beverly Hills 90210*—a show about *hiau* girls and guys where all they care about is BGR and popularity stuff. That show is so so so popular with everyone! Jason Priestley and Luke Perry are the main idols. The way *All Stars* write about them makes my blood boil: "Luke may be a big celebrity now but deep down inside, he's still the same", "You girls out there who are gaga over Luke Perry, do not be heart-broken that he has a girlfriend, you can still do things like read these facts we have about him." Then they ask you to daydream that you and Luke are in certain situations: you're on the beach, all the girls are crazy about him but he only has eyes for you ... Then they have pages and pages of stupid articles about Luke and Jason and pictures of them, some hugging Shannon Doherty (of *Beverly Hills*). I bet some fanatical fans will be so envious. Then there's this interview where girls can ask questions about Jeremy Miller (Ben of *Growing Pains*). This is what *All Stars* says: "You loving fans out there can be pleased to know that when the girls asked the question 'Do you have a girlfriend', he proclaimed that he is still handsomely single ..." Aargh. Aargh. Aargh again. I think it's all so silly. I can just imagine all those adoring fans buying the mag and reading and reading then staring at the posters and going so crazy! *All Stars* always tells you just a little bit of info so you'll buy more issues. And they make a BIG DEAL out of Luke drinking a drink or doing something mundane. So Stupid. OK, OK, I shouldn't get all worked up about all this. It doesn't concern me, of course.

I finished my essay on Van Gogh. Yeah! Four pages.

Studying in Singapore makes me think that life is not so meaningful if all you do is study, study and get good results. I mean, so what if someone is so clever?

And yesterday, I was bothered 'coz people here are so selfish about their studies. I can't stand it when people pretend they're lazy and not working. I mean, what's wrong with being hardworking.

Alisa has this thing about beauty. She only eats fruits for recess, she never eats during dinner. She just eats a little veg and a few spoonfuls of rice! It's terrible. Yesterday, she jogged round the track ten times. She tells people she eats A LOT but actually, Nancy says she never eats.

It's now 12.10 am. Oh no, I forgot to bathe today!
Love, Pei Yi

Tuesday 28 April

Dear Mei Yee
Hi! Hi! Hi! AEP exam was OK. There were some questions I couldn't answer. Imagine, just seconds before the exam, I skimmed through that page which had the answers but I didn't pay any attention to the name of that person (whom I thought unimportant) and it came up!

I wish I was in Science class 'coz for Chem, they're learning all these complicated things. I've all sorts of questions like HCl is ionic or covalent bonding, draw SO_2 bonding etc, which Jen Nee can't answer. If I ask my teacher, she'll say it's out of the syllabus. Anyway, I can't explain what I'm saying. It's just that I feel if I was in the Science class, I could do better than them. Once they were talking about a Physics question and although they're in Science class, I don't think they're cleverer. It's just that my syllabus is less and simpler. And furthermore the subjects I find difficult are Arts subjects, not Science subjects.

Oh ya, Gaik Teong gave us an IQ question that he can't solve. Alisa, Jen Nee and I tried to do it. They couldn't, but I could!! I was so happy 'coz I thought and thought. I hope I don't sound like I'm boasting.
Love, Pei Yi

Mei Yee, Hi! Today I didn't study. After AEP, I played badminton with Jen Nee then sang *Miss Saigon* with her. Prep (read Chem and came up with thousands of questions) then did the IQ question. Now I'm writing to you. Do you think it's a waste, me not going to Science class? Well, actually it's not that I want to learn Physics and Chem that much, but I just want to get good marks for subjects that people don't. No, no, no. Maybe I won't even get good marks. Never mind. I'm writing rubbish so

I'd better say bye.
Pei Yi

Thursday 30 April

Dearest Mei Yee
Just came back from school. Received your letter.

This whole week Jen Nee and I woke up so late that we've been reaching school a minute before the bell rings or during assembly. Luckily, we haven't been booked yet. Yesterday after prep, Jen Nee asked me to tell Gaik Teong I can do the IQ question 'coz he can't do it. So funny.

This Sat is my heart checkup. I asked my dad NOT to come but he wants to 'coz he's so anxious to know. Betty (who's tall) says she also has some heart problem (it occurs in too thin or tall people) but it's not harmful to health. I just don't know what I'm going to be next time, whether I'll have a bright future or not.

I'll end now as I've exams coming. BYE.
Love, Pei Yi
PS Tell me about training camp. Who showed good leadership qualities, who likes who etc?

Saturday 2 May

Dear Mei Yee
Hi! This morning my dad came and we took a taxi to Tan Tock Seng Hospital. The doctor was VERY nice and friendly. She listened to my heart. I had an x-ray and ECG. She said my heart has a clicking sound (an extra sound) but there's no back-flow so there's nothing to worry 'bout. She said everyone is built differently. Anyway, I still have to do an echogram to confirm everything. I was SO happy there's nothing wrong with my heart.
Love, Pei Yi

Tuesday 4 May

Dear Mei Yee

I read *Teenage* today. This month, the four girls in the makeover looked WORSE after the makeover! One of Johnny Depp's fans sent him her pubic hair!! And there was an article 'bout girls chasing guys. The guys say they'd be very flattered—boosting their egos, as usual. There are so many good and funny Singaporean writers. I always laugh when I read their articles.

Love Pei Yi

Tuesday 12 May

Hi Mei Yee!

History exam today. We had to write four essays in two hours. As I've sort of memorized some and we knew which essays to prepare that might come out, it was quite easy. I was so silly. The exam was supposed to end at 9.40 am but for some reason I thought it was supposed to end at 9.20 am! So at 9 am I began writing so fast that my hand was SO tense and my writing was quite untidy. I finished at 9.15 am then only realized my mistake!

The guys are so crazy over the badminton Thomas Cup matches. Matt went to watch TV after prep and then he came and told me about it. He was so excited 'bout Malaysia winning. Actually I didn't know what he was talking about 'coz I don't watch sports. The RI Maths standard is really very high. The guys (like Gaik Teong, Matt, Cheng Hoe) are really great at Maths. Yesterday I had this log question which I spent a lot of time on and couldn't do so I asked Gaik Teong:

$$2^{x+1} - 3^{2x-1} = 2^x$$

Cheng Hoe did it. And it was so funny, 'coz Nancy came and wanted to interfere. She said, "What! Why you so dumb one?!" and "You confuse me!" to Cheng Hoe. Then Gaik Teong (who's VERY funny) said, "Wah! Nancy is confused by Cheng Hoe! Cheng Hoe, you're so attractive!" I laughed and laughed 'coz the guys are very funny. I don't know how they can be so funny.

My dream is to get top place for Add. Maths and but this is very difficult for me to achieve. I've never had such aspirations before. I mean, last time, all I thought about was guys. Jen Nee is still studying for her Chem exam and it's now 12.45 am. Last night, we studied till 2 am, reciting History essays to each other. Jen Nee studies last minute but she spends a lot of time on each chapter 'coz she pays attention to every detail! I'm so carefree about exams. For example if I have History test tomorrow, I'll do Add. Maths. Actually, I hardly study.

Jen Nee and me have a devious plan. We laughed and laughed about it: we're going to be hardworking, doing our Maths secretly after the exams when everyone else is having fun, so we'll be cleverer than them. Ha! Ha! Love, Pei Yi

Wednesday 13 May

Hi, it's 10 pm and we're waiting for the warden to check our rooms. They want to see whether we're neat.

Tomorrow is the Add. Maths exam. The Physics exam was very easy. But everyone else was moaning and groaning. Aargh, I'm feeling so bored right now. Can't wait till exams are over. Now, I don't know what I'm interested in and what I want to be.

I haven't gone to any movies since Feb! Last year I went 12 times. I love going to movies.

Hi! It's now 1 am. I just watched the Thomas Cup. Did you watch it? It was so exciting!!! At 12.30 am the TV went off so we rushed up to a warden's room to watch. I'm so proud of Malaysia!! Everyone is!

Just now, Nicole, Elizabeth, Jen Nee and I watched *Father of the Bride* at the cinema. It was very touching, very funny. Matt said he tried not to cry but he did. I cried throughout the show because the father in the movie reminded me of my dad. Wish my dad could have seen the show too.

Matt invited us to go to McDs to celebrate Cheng Hoe's birthday tomorrow morning.

Elizabeth is going on a Creative Arts camp, where they teach creative writing and stuff. I want to go! But you have to be selected by your school, apply or something like that.
Love, Pei Yi

Sunday 17 May

Dear Mei Yee
Hi! In the morning, Jen Nee, Elizabeth, Matt, Cheng Hoe (birthday boy) and I went to McD for breakfast. When we came back, we each made Cheng Hoe a card. They took ideas from my book where I write the card stuff. Then we gave them to Cheng Hoe. This card is so funny—in front it reads: "This card can only be opened by someone kind, helpful, friendly, handsome, athletic ..." and Cheng Hoe looked so flattered. Then he tried and tried to open the card while we laughed and laughed. At the back, it says, "Don't tell me you even tried!"

Jen Nee said it's not that fun going to McD with those guys 'coz there's not much of interest to talk about. She said she's more comfortable with Gaik Teong 'coz he's very funny. I enjoyed going to McD with them though. Oh ya, I think I unintentionally embarrassed Matt just now 'coz I asked him at which part of *Father of the Bride* he cried.

Went swimming with Jen Nee. I felt VERY frustrated 'coz I still can't swim! It's been five months! I'm abnormal.

Saw Matt at night and talked to him. He had to sit in the hostel office beside the assistant manager and study because he came back after the curfew last night.

Love, Pei Yi

Dear Mei Yee

OK. I've been feeling miserable about my class. I had the opportunity to choose Science classes. I didn't and I regret it. I don't know why I chose A4. Ignorance, I guess. I didn't really think that A4 would be a lousy class. I just thought of the subject combinations. And at that time, I wanted to be an accountant but I'm not so sure now. I'm very bothered 'coz I still don't know what to be and I'm already fifteen. I know it's no use crying over spilt milk. If it were you, you'd make the best out of what you had and not regret anything, right? And what if I want to be become something that needs science subjects but I can't? I don't know. I just keep feeling miserable 'bout it every waking moment! Also, I realized that I'm a person who tends to dwell on the past too much. I mean, I keep thinking if I'd done this and that, now I'd be happier, and if this had happened instead etc. Jen Nee says I dwell on the past too much.

The reason I say my class is lousy is 'coz they got such poor results in the mid-year exams. My marks were much, much higher than theirs—I'm not terribly pleased about that because it means that I'm not being challenged. I feel that they sort of have a common bond 'coz they get about the same marks. Can you understand what I mean? Never mind. I must get into a good junior college next time. I wish people had not intimidated me 'bout the standard of education here. It was partly the fear that I would not have been able to catch up which made my dad influence me to enter the Arts stream.

I think another reason I'm feeling terrible is that the Singapore *kiasuism* is getting to me badly. Every one of the scholars is becoming so clever while I'm stagnated, trapped and totally out-of-place in my class. I can't identify with any of my classmates; not that I want to. I know this class-problem will be solved when I go to a good JC but then I would've wasted two years of my precious teen life being unhappy, and not learning as much as I could have.

Elizabeth and I had a long talk after school. She said her class (in RGS) is really *kiasu*. One girl even wrote an essay "How To Make Your Friend Not Study". Can you believe it? That's so terrible. The methods are stealing her notes (!!!), phoning her, making her stay back in school, telling her, "It's very easy, you can finish it all in one night", and telling her, "I haven't studied at all". I think it's all really stupid. Some of them go round asking, "What are you doing now? Have you studied this or that?"

Elizabeth and I went downstairs to the lounge and Leo came along so we asked the sissy to tell us about "a day in RI". His class is shocking. They talk about marks and positions all the time. They even snatched the results from the teacher's hands when she said, "I'll tell you later." His friend suggested stealing his rival Alfred's notes so that he wouldn't be able to study. And Leo pesters the teacher for 1 meager mark so that he can beat Alfred. According to him, Alfred beat him by 0.6 marks so he needs 0.7 marks to beat him! When the school bell rings, all the boys RUN back home to study. I think he's exaggerating a bit but for some people, *kiasuism* is really evident. Then Elizabeth turned to Leo and said, "So, you rushed home to talk to us, is it?" Leo quickly jumped up, said he had to study and ran off, and our pleas to ask him to stay fell on deaf ears.

People try to take the maximum number of subjects so that they reach their full potential and also try to take more subjects than everyone else. I mean, since we all have 24 hours a day, if someone can learn one more subject than everyone else, it's like they are ahead. So someone will boast that they take AEP, Higher Chinese or German as an extra subject while they are already taking all the hard subjects in the Science class. I keep thinking how I can spend my time optimally. I'm afraid that my brain will atrophy since I'm not maximizing it.

The other day, Jen Nee and I went to the SPCA to do volunteer work. It was fun, though nothing to do with animals. In fact I didn't even see any animals. We stacked booklets and papers into piles. Then I joined as a member for S$5 and bought a dog poster for S$1. I found S$3 on the way there so I donated that to the SPCA. We took one and a half hours to get to the SPCA 'coz of a little kid. First we got on Bus 152, which I knew went to the SPCA but I didn't know where to stop so I asked the bus driver. He didn't even know what SPCA was. Then a little Malay boy told us that he knows and that his father works there. I asked, as what? He replied, "Sandiwara". Anyway we followed his directions, took Bus 231 and ended up in God-knows-where. Then we realized that he thought we meant SBC (Singapore Broadcasting Corp.), and "Sandiwara" is a Malay movie. So we took Bus 152 again and this bus driver was even more irritating 'coz he kept asking why we wanted to go to *kou he mau* (dog and cat).

Bye!
Love, Pei Yi

4
Eric

Monday 25 May

Dear Mei Yee
Today we got more results:

> History 75% (I'm so happy)
> Add. Maths 88% only (my dreams are shattered—someone
>   from another class got 94%)
> E. Maths 93% (Jen Nee and Alisa got lower than me for both Maths)
> Accounts 97%.

I think I'm top in my class for everything.

My Batchlings are organizing this year's Farewell for Sec 4s on 18 July.
Jen Nee, Eric (he looks like Alvin the Chipmunk) and I are in charge of
deco (decorations). Last night, Jen Nee and I discussed what to do. I was
so enthusiastic 'bout it. Imagine, everyone looking at our deco the whole
night!

Today I wrote a short story. At last, a successful story (with a steamy
scene). I'm sending it to *The Student Today*.
Love, Pei Yi

Thursday 28 May

Dear Mei Yee
Tomorrow is a BIG day for me. It might just change the REST of my life. I made a sudden decision—I'm going to ask Mrs Simons and Sister Elaine to let me change to Science 3. I really want to go. I feel I can cope with the extra work and can beat the girls there in Physics, Chem and Maths. I hope I get to change. All my hopes in my life will depend on TOMORROW.
Love, Pei Yi

Friday 29 May

Dear Mei Yee
I couldn't sleep till about 4 am thinking about how I'll make my argument to Mrs Simons and Sister Elaine. I wrote down all my points on a piece of paper. I said I wasn't being challenged, my full potential is not being reached, all the ASEAN scholars are in Science classes, what if I want to be a doctor in the future, I had the chance to choose a Science class at the beginning of the year but made the wrong choice, etc. I was so nervous yet hopeful when I went to talk to them.

Well, their reply was: NO—I can't go to 3S3. I should have known. Sister Elaine says it's not fair to the others—they can't give me special treatment. She says all the parents of the Arts classes will also ask for a change if she allows me to switch classes.

My dad came to my school. He and his two friends are on holiday driving down from BM. He felt sad that he had asked me to go to Arts class but I told him it's my own fault for not finding out more about the differences between Arts and Science classes. Anyway, I promised him that I'll be happy staying in 3A4 and will make the best of it. I'm trying to convince myself that being in my class is a blessing in disguise. I try to think of the pros instead of the cons. My sister used to think that pros and cons meant prostitutes and conmen.

Anyway, the pros are:

1 Besides learning Physics and Chem, I also learn Accounts
2 It's a chance for me to learn to be on my own (not being in the same class as hostel friends)
3 A wider circle of friends
4 Gives me incentive to do well in Add. Maths 'coz I want to prove that being in an Arts class doesn't mean you're even more stupid

I hate Sister Elaine.

My goals are:

1 Memorize all History essays
2 Do Add. Maths till confident can beat Science classes
3 Read Chemistry till perfect
4 Do all the above

Love, Pei Yi

Sunday 14 June (*Back home in BM!*)

Mei Yee!
I'm so used to writing to you that I'm writing even at home! Slept the whole day 'coz of diorhrea (can't spell). Will see you tomorrow.
Love, Pei Yi

Monday 15 June

Dear Mei Yee
I had diorhrea again. And still can't spell it. So sad had to postpone our plan till tomorrow.
Love, Pei Yi

Saturday 27 June (*Back from Malaysia*)

Dear Mei Yee
Hi! It's 2.30 am. I miss home and family and you. I hope I get over it soon. Right now I feel my life is being divided into two, one part in BM and one here. Why can't I have both together?

Found out that a few others in my hostel who went back to Malaysia also had diorhrea (still can't spell)! I guess our immune systems lose their strength in Singapore! diarrhoea dioreah
Love, Pei Yi

Sunday 28 June

Hi! It's now prep time. Must they have it even before school starts?!
You know, I used to feel angry about people selling their stuff at inflated prices to foreigners 'coz it's cheating. Well, I don't anymore 'coz now I realize that they need to survive and also most people's attitude in life is to only care 'bout themselves and their families. And even though some people seem respectable and all, it's actually only a façade. After reading *The Inspector Calls*, I think it's very true. I think a lot of businessmen are greedy and selfish, and they cheat. Jen Nee told me her mother sometimes bluffs that the goods are from Japan so that the buyer will buy. Everyone in this world seems so terrible. Maybe now we don't think so 'coz we're not really exposed yet but probably we will when we're working.
Pei Yi

Monday 29 June

Dear Mei Yee
I read in the *Sunday Mail* about an old woman in England buying framed photos of Elvis Presley to rub his private part. They claim that it has healing powers and some even claimed to be cured! Isn't that preposterous?

Teens has given me no reply 'bout the freelance writer stuff. I must try to use more difficult words so please tolerate my trying to use bombastic words in my letters.

Mrs Simons said American magazines like *Newsweek* and *Time* are very misleading 'coz they are not neutral. They try to influence you to their point of view, for example how they describe Saddam Hussein. I think America always appears to be so saintly but they actually do things to their advantage. But of course everyone does that.
Love, Pei Yi

Tuesday 30 June

Dear Mei Yee

Hi! I'm out of my blue mood now. Serena, my classmate, gave me a box of chocolates 'coz she visited USA during the hols. I'm beginning to enjoy school now that I have nice classmates. (No, not because they gave me chocolates.)

Oh ya, everyone was excited about the chewing gum that I brought them. I was afraid that the people at Customs would question me about the packs of chewing gum but they didn't.

Now our canteen, in fact every school's canteen, is not permitted to sell certain soft drinks and junk food. I think the Singapore government is always concerned 'bout the progress of the nation.

I've finished writing a ghost story. Sometimes I get very afraid when I think about the supernatural, especially when it's dark.

I read a book 'bout spelling. Now I can spell diarrhoea, manoeuvre, miscellaneous and lots more. I really want to be very figurative in my writing so I can paint a picture for the reader.
Love, Pei Yi

Thursday 2 July

Dear Mei Yee

My ghost story turned out to be most unscary. In fact, Huiwee said it was rather comical. I wonder why and how sometimes the ghost stories we read can be so scary, even if the story seems so preposterous. Dean R. Koontz's novels are very "out of this world" but still very exciting and thrilling.

Did I tell you, Mrs Simons is going on a Maths course until April of next year. There'll be a substitute teacher in her place. I hope he or she is as good as Mrs Simons. She makes Maths so interesting and enjoyable. But not all CHIJ teachers are that great. Who says Singapore education is perfect?

Cheng Hoe is so funny 'coz he is so blur and dense. Last night he went to Jen Nee's table. He saw a picture that Jen Nee drew of me. Eric guessed it was me and Jen Nee even said, "Yes, it's Pei Yi." Cheng Hoe still said, "Let me guess." Even though Jen Nee told him once again the sketch was of me, he still looked like he wanted to guess!
Love, Pei Yi

Dearest Mei Yee

Tonight, Eric, Jen Nee and I did deco. It was great fun. Sunny helped us do the lettering. Alisa is being so bossy and irritating though. She thinks that she and Pau Leen are the only ones to put any effort into Farewell. She implies this when she speaks and she wants to take all the credit. Pau Leen is equally bossy. She's already the MC and she's also a rep for Farewell but she wants to take over everything else as well. She wants us to follow her ideas for deco but we're not going to. I wish I could show you everything.

My God, it's 3 am now! Must sleep.
Love, Pei Yi

Sunday 5 July

Dear Mei Yee

Today was a very fun day! In the morning we did deco. We've finished the painting. It was fun doing it. Eric is very knowledgeable about art. He's the RI Networking Club president and he looks like Alvin the Chipmunk—so cute. I talked more to him, and I'm glad about it.

There are so many places to visit in Singapore, like the zoo, the libraries, the ice-skating ring, Orchard Road. The libraries are full of people reading, they're not empty like the ones in Malaysia.

The *Teenage* Centrefold Girl (July issue) is such a spoilt *loh heng* brat. She goes shopping twice a week, spending more than S$200 each time! She is doted on by her father and relatives and she's extremely brand-conscious. If her friends have any branded goods, she'll make sure that she gets the same or better straightaway. This seems to be a common Singaporean trait. She wants to be a model, that *loh heng*-faced girl!

Glossary
loh heng Hokkien hateful appearance, a person who inspires hate

---

I think Eric's a very nice guy. He has a cute grin and he blinks his eyes like when you don't believe what you see and he wears specs. He was Alisa's classmate in Malaysia. We were surprised to hear he's president of Networking Club 'coz he looks quite quiet and innocent from the outside. Although he seems so proper (he even says "Good morning" and "Good night"), I think he's fun. I wish he'd like me. Ya, it sounds silly but I do. OK, to make Eric like me, I must talk more to him. I must appear cheerful and interesting.

Gaik Teong likes Nancy, we think. He said he's not going to the Farewell but when Jen Nee said, "Nancy is going," he replied, "Then I'm going." He might not be serious, being the crazy person that he is, but he once said Nancy is beautiful.

I bet people like Eric never worry about shallow stuff like popularity. Why do I? I think Jen Nee's very sociable. People often tease her a lot— a sign that she's liked. I must know more 'bout everything 'coz every time people talk 'bout songs, actors and movies, I don't know anything.
Love, Pei Yi

Dear Mei Yee
My Maths teacher, Mrs Simons, has left for her course. She'll only be back in April next year! Mr Koh, the substitute teacher, is so boring.

My horoscope this week is so correct! It says that I'll have frustrations in the middle of the week (true!) but I'll have fun and enjoyment at the end of the week (at the Farewell, I hope). The frustrations were: Sunny is so unreasonable. She got angry with Jen Nee and me 'coz she said we're irresponsible and left the deco lettering to her. But it was she who said she wants to do everything. She went to tell Alisa about it! I was so angry with her. Jen Nee and I went to have a "talk" with Sunny but nothing really turned out right. Aargh, everything's so upsetting. I wonder if Sunny will now go talk bad about Jen Nee and I behind our backs. Since she used to talk bad about others to us, she might talk bad about us now that she is angry with us.

Bye
love, Pei Yi

Thursday 9 July

Dear Mei Yee
Pau Leen and Alisa really overdid it pestering us! Yesterday and today they kept pestering, as if they have absolutely no faith in our capability. I was so mad at them. And quite cross with Eric 'coz he never gets the pestering. All the responsibilities are dumped on me and Jen Nee while Eric enjoys himself. After Toa Payoh Central, we came back to the hostel and paged for Eric to force him to carry the Styrofoam with us. Jen Nee said, "We must make you suffer," and I said, "We always do the

work," and we told him about Pau Leen and Alisa's pestering. Eric said he understands what it's like to be pestered by Alisa.

Earlier, Alisa had asked me how we're going to put the picture on the Styrofoam. I said use Sellotape and she replied, "Cannot lah, blah, blah, blah", but I insisted "can" and she said, "You all, don't be so relaxed, lah!" Later I asked Eric and he said to use tape so I told him what Alisa said to my suggestion of using tape. Eric said if I need help convincing Alisa about it, ask him 'coz he can threaten to spread rumours about Alisa. I was surprised that he said things like that 'coz outwardly he looks so serious.

Anyway, tomorrow we're supposed to put up deco and other stuff for Farewell in my school hall. So I asked Eric to meet me at the bus interchange at 2.45 pm. Then just now, Pau Leen came to talk to Jen Nee, and now Pau Leen wants to go and meet Eric. It was so obvious that Pau Leen wanted to be the one to take him to our school. I couldn't say I want to meet him 'coz she asked me this way, "I'll go meet him since I'm going to Toa Payoh Central unless you really want to go meet him." Anyway, why all this fuss about meeting him?

Eric seems to know how to go 'bout doing everything. For example for drawing the huge circle he said, use a string, someone hold it down in the middle, then draw. And lots of other things. And yesterday, Jen Nee was cutting Styrofoam with a blade and the flakes were flying and sticking to her shirt. Eric said something 'bout static electricity and how it can be solved by putting a piece of Styrofoam underneath the piece you're cutting. He's so scientific yet so sociable. He's the RI Inventors Club vice-president and Networking Club president.

I should really sleep now. It's 2.10 am. Yesterday, Lucy, Nicole, Jen Nee and I did the lettering for deco till 2.30 am while Eric was probably sleeping like a log. Now I've so many things to do. Things to study, storybooks, AEP project etc but I think I like it when it's busy like this. I feel like I'm not wasting any time because I'm always doing something.

I feel like I need more than 24 hours a day.

Love, Pei Yi

Sunday 12 July

Dear Mei Yee

Yesterday's Farewell was great. I had a lot of fun. The deco was a success. The Sec 4s loved it. Betty remarked it was one of the best they've ever had. I had a lot of fun dancing 'coz I tried to *taruh sajalah*, and not bother if it looked nice or not.

Glossary

taruh sajalah *Malay* just do it

The Farewell was held in my school hall. Jen Nee and I went to finish the deco at noon. Alisa, being her usual self, clapped her hands sarcastically when we arrived, 'coz she thought we should have been there earlier.

There were quite a few performances. Ours was a play where we reconstructed the scene when we were having meetings to discuss the Farewell items. It was very funny. Matt and Pratesh (an Indian) danced a very funny dance.

We bought roses for the seniors. But Gaik Teong bought one for Nancy. First he asked Nancy, "Do you like roses?" Nancy, who's always mean to him, said, "No!" We forced him to give her the rose. He pretended to mumble some made-up form of "Eenie meenie mynie moe" pointing to us and then Nancy but of course ended up pointing at Nancy. Nancy accepted it at last.

Overall everything was fun but unfortunately, something was quite disappointing for me—no one asked me to slow-dance. Maybe it's 'coz Jen Nee and I had to do classroom duties for half an hour and it was during that half hour that they had slow-dancing but what if it wasn't because of that? I told Jen Nee I was bothered about why no one asked me to dance; is something wrong with me? Jen Nee said even if no one asks her to dance, she doesn't think that she's abnormal. Eric danced with many girls.

After the Farewell, Jen Nee and me "gossiped" and talked about relationships among the hostelites.

Jen Nee and I think that guys are so ignorant of girls' true colours 'coz they only see the outward side of girls, while girls can see the real side of girls. Alisa and Pau Leen must seem very nice to them. Likewise, Matt and Eric might turn out to be horrible people.

The other day, Jen Nee and I were in Toa Payoh when we saw a skinny, black, stray kitten. It looked so pitiful so I asked Jen Nee to buy it a McFillet while I watched it. While she was gone, the kitten stayed at my feet and then a petite, quite old woman came up to me and asked if it was my cat. She wanted to take it to a safer place. We found out that she carries baskets of rice and other food everyday to feed stray cats. She says she feeds 80 cats a day! She disapproves of sending cats to the SPCA 'coz they'll be put to sleep there. She said, people think she's crazy but she doesn't care. What an experience meeting someone like that! I can hardly believe it. She must be a bit crazy. But she's not doing the cats good, as she thinks she is, because this will only lead to more stray cats living terrible lives. The best thing to do is to put them to sleep. I just don't understand how people can mistreat vulnerable cats and dogs by throwing stones at them or kicking them! She witnessed a lot of those things.

This Wednesday, I'm going to visit a centre for ex-lepers with the Social Work Unit of my school. I wish I had joined the LDDS (Literature, Drama and Debating Society) in my school and also Networking Club ('coz you get to socialize with other schools) but I guess you can't have everything.

Sometimes when nice things happen to your friends, do you feel happy

for them or jealous? Sometimes I feel the latter but I'm trying to get rid of that attitude. For example if Jen Nee gets paired up with, let's say, Cheng Hoe, Matt or Eric, and I'm alone, I guess I'll be jealous.
Love, Pei Yi

Wednesday 15 July

Dear Mei Yee
The 13th was Eric's birthday. He's fifteen. Jen Nee, Nicole and I bought him a birthday card. He replied with a very funny letter. Jen Nee drew Alvin the Chipmunk on the envelope. He thought that Alisa told us 'bout him looking like Alvin the Chipmunk. It seems that he was nicknamed Alvin even in Malaysia. So we were not the only ones to notice. So funny.

Today was Choir Club election. Nancy became President. I hope we'll have more performances 'coz Nancy puts her heart into the Choir Club. Another girl, Bee Kay, and I were nominated for pianist. Each of us had to sight-read this Prelude No. 2 by Gershwin 'coz at first they asked me to play anything but I couldn't 'coz I didn't have any notes. Anyway, the sight-reading was terrible 'coz it didn't really have any tune but I tried to pretend to be confident. I heard from Jen Nee that Bee Kay's playing was even worse 'coz she seemed very uncertain and nervous. I was SO glad to be pianist 'coz after my sight-reading I was quite worried. I don't know whether it's true or not, but Bee Kay kept saying she was so happy 'coz she actually doesn't want to be pianist. There are too few members in our Choir Club. It's not a very good club. I was playing a song for them to sing, and the lyrics had the word refrain in between the verses. Bee Kay said it meant the singers are to refrain from singing at those sections!

After that, I went with the Social Work Unit to the ex-lepers' home. The residents were aged above 65. They looked so pitiful 'coz they are disfigured. Some have amputated limbs and deformed faces. We talked to them. The way old people talk is very difficult to understand. They speak in dialects and they mumble. We watched them weave baskets and sew. I bought a cosmetics pouch although I don't need one.

Mr Koh (the substitute Maths teacher) is TERRIBLE. I argued with him 'coz he was teaching wrongly. I'm now convinced that he is absolutely hopeless in Maths. During Maths period, my blood boils. O how I miss Mrs Simons! 3S1 has already finished every question in the textbook and 10 Year Series for that chapter while we're still at the beginning. The thing is, he can't teach 'coz he himself doesn't understand. I have complained enough to Jen Nee and Alisa so I'm going to solve this problem by depending on myself. But it's going to be very difficult to beat 3S1; they have Mr Tan, who's a Maths genius. Mr Koh really makes me feel SO frustrated.
Love, Pei Yee

Dear Mei Yee
I was so happy to receive your letter. Thank you. It was very amusing and interesting.

Today I argued with Mr Koh the Maths teacher 'coz he taught wrongly again. Although I had never learned that chapter before, I knew that it was wrong. He was so un-Maths-teacher-like to say that $p = 180$ degrees. Where got such thing? Actually it has something to do with radian but he said, no need to explain. I showed my classmates the letter I wrote to him (which I had at first decided not to give him) but they all agreed and we gave him the letter. My class is very fed up with him 'coz when we ask him why, and what's the proof of the formula, he said, no need proof, cannot be proven, last time long time ago people already said it's like that so we must follow. Then I figured out how to prove it by myself. After that lesson, he wanted to talk to me so I told him all the things I disliked about him (without being rude). I guess there's nothing that can be done. He said he tries his best, but he has not touched Maths for two years. His deplorable state of mind cannot be improved. So I've to depend on myself. It's 'coz he did not understand properly that he cannot remember. This problem of Mr Koh is bugging me. But at least I've told him. He read the very straightforward letter I wrote in front of me. At least he didn't get angry. Well, I guess it's not his fault that he's stupid. I must ask my classmates to be kinder to him.

The way Singaporeans pronounce Genting Highlands is so weird! The G is not hard as in "god"—as it should be—but soft as in "gender"! Also they've never heard of the expression "new pinch!"

Glossary

Genting Highlands vacation resort in Malaysia
new pinch saying "new pinch!" while pinching someone when they have a new possession

---

Although Alisa's class (3S3) doesn't like Mr Koh also, they pretend to be very nice to him. Some of them even think Mrs Simons is not very good at teaching. I think Mrs Simons is closer to my class than theirs. There're many lively, energetic, spontaneous girls in my class. I'm glad I told Mr Koh all that I felt 'bout his teaching methods and wasting time. If he improves a little bit, isn't it great for 3S3 who didn't have to do anything? Maybe I should just let things happen and not make them happen.

I want to be good at Maths. It's not fair, me having such a lousy teacher and 3S1 having Mr Tan! To beat the girl in that class with the highest Add. Maths marks, I've got to score 100 for final year exams and she has to get below 94 'coz she got 94 in the mid-year exam and I got 88. Wow, your Maths is good. I think you can excel in many fields if given the opportunity.

Well, I've spent too much time writing. I think I'm the only one in the hostel to write so much. Reply soon and BYE.
Love, Pei Yi

Sunday 19 July

Dear Mei Yee
I just posted a letter to you two days ago but I'm writing again 'coz if I

don't, by the time I receive your reply, I would have forgotten what I wanted to tell you.

Yesterday, I didn't eat for the whole day! You see, Nancy, Jen Nee and I are participating in the 30-hour Famine. We don't eat, then we sell coupons to people to raise funds for the starving people in Ethiopia. We knew 'bout this from the man from Ethiopia who gave us a talk. I was so hungry. We are allowed to drink, fortunately. Today I woke up early to have the long-waited-for breakfast. How terrible it must be to be an Ethiopian. They go without food for months, then die of starvation!

The other night, Jen Nee and I were telling ghost stories. Jen Nee has once experienced the presence of spirits. She was alone at home, and her hand on its own tried to touch herself against her will. She tried to control it. All these stories are SO frightening! I was surprised to find that Jen Nee has the same fear as me—looking into a mirror and seeing something other than your reflection.

I think Maths is such a beautiful subject 'coz it's so logical and so extremely clever! I think too many people do not relate Maths to real things. They just work the questions out and get some figures that have no meaning. For example when some of my classmates solve quadratic equations they don't know what it really is or how the curve looks like. Sometimes I don't' really understand everything but I try to. I'm going to do homework now.

Bye
Love, Pei Yi
PS Alisa took the opportunity to starve herself 'for the 30-hour Famine but she's not asking for donations, she just wanted to slim down!

Tuesday 21 July

Dear Mei Yee
I just finished talking to my family on the phone. I told my mum about

Mr Koh and my letter to him, and she actually scolded me for being rude to him. She said that she and my dad have had bad experiences with students who think that they're so smart and who are disrespectful to them, and she was disappointed in me for the way I handled it. Gosh, now I feel really bad. I am going to make a real effort to be nicer to him at class.

Love, Pei Yei

Wednesday 29 July

Dear Mei Yee

I'm going to enter a chess competition in my school. I hope I can beat at least a few people. I've been playing with Nicole, who claimed that she was an expert and that she has never lost since Primary 5. But it turned out that she wasn't really good. I beat her in five out of seven games.

Recently, Leo (the Sec 1 sissy) has been teasing me with Eric. He also went to ask Eric if "there's anything going on between me and him" and Eric responded with his famous Alvin the Chipmunk grin. I was pretty embarrassed about it when I knew that he asked this in case Eric thinks that I like him. Well, actually, I could like him, but I don't want to 'coz I don't think he'll like me. You know, like you say, control your feelings and it won't become an infatuation.

We know Ekan gave a girl a rose during Farewell and we deduced that it was Alisa. Jen Nee and I bugged Eric to tell us but he won't 'coz he has promised Ekan to keep it a secret. When I bugged him further, Eric asked me, "You can keep a secret, right?" I replied, "Ya". He said, "So can I!" Afterwards, I was quite bothered in case he thinks I'm a gossip and a *sampat* and don't respect Ekan's privacy. Jen Nee said, if the situation were reversed, I wouldn't have a bad impression of him, so don't worry. You know the Sustagen advertisement on TV last time? The voice of Geno was Wah Yi, a Sec 4 guy now. He was in Primary 4 then. He said he had to sing again and again for a month for one ad! When I said, "Hi, Geno!" to him, he thought that I said, "Hi, gigolo!"

> **Glossary**
> **sampat** localized Malaysian/Singaporean spelling of the Mandarin slang "*san ba*" meaning crazy and/or unrefined person
> **Sustagen** an energy drink for kids promoted by two child characters, Susie and Geno

Thursday 30 July

Dear Mei Yee

Hi again! Just now, I was in the newspaper room. I asked Sunny to play chess with me but she didn't want to. She asked me to ask Gaik Teong, who was nearby, so I did. I think guys are terrible 'coz they can't bear the thought of losing to girls. Gaik Teong was very reluctant to play until I convinced him that I'm a beginner. I borrowed this chess book from library but I haven't read it 'coz it looks very boring. Anyway, Matt came along so I asked him to play instead since Gaik Teong kept trying to give excuses not to play. Matt asked whether I'm an amateur 'coz he said it'll "hurt his ego" if he loses. Can you believe that?! Ego. Ego. I can't stand it. I told him I'm a beginner and that I need to practice 'coz I signed up for a competition. Cheng Hoe gave me a tip or two 'coz I made bad opening moves. While Gaik Teong, Sunny and Alisa were socializing, we played chess. I won and then wished I hadn't 'coz Matt looked disappointed and ashamed. No one (I mean guys) will want to play with me again. Jen Nee said it's stupid to care 'bout that—why must they always win?

I just played chess with Nancy. I won. She's a good sport and she said I can play with her anytime I want. Nicole doesn't want to play anymore 'coz she loses most of the time. I'm going to ask Mr Koh to play chess with me. He's actually not that bad. I mean, he's still bad at teaching Maths, but I realize that he's really trying his best, and he's not a bad person.

When I think back on how mean I was to Mr Koh (in May), I feel quite remorseful. It was unfair of me to be judgmental towards him. Even though his Maths is not as good as Mr Tan, it doesn't give me the right to be rude to him. In fact, it was very gracious of him to listen to my "letter of complaint" without getting angry. I talked to Huiwee, Lingling and Serena about this and they said that they'll ask our other classmates to be more respectful of him.

I'm reading acopy of *The Roman World* from the library. Can you believe that I actually like History a little now? I used to despise, loathe, hate and dislike it extremely back in BM. We're going on a History trip to Malacca on 21 August and we'll be staying in a very posh hotel. I like Mrs Jean (History teacher). She's very sweet. You know, like that kind of sweet, pleasant, kind European lady.
Love, Pei Yi

Saturday 1 August

Dear Mei Yee
Hello! (For a change.) Yesterday I received your letter. I giggled and giggled while reading it.

Elizabeth's a great chess player. She taught me some things. I must finish reading the chess book.
Love, Pei Yi

Sunday 2 August

Dear Mei Yee
This afternoon, Jen Nee and I watched a free orchestral performance at the Botanical Gardens. The AYO (Asian Youth Orchestra) performed. These people are so lucky. They get to go around the world to perform. And they have Sir Yehudin Menuhin as the music director. There were many spectators. All of us sat on the grass. There were many Caucasians. The family and friends sitting beside us were having a picnic on a mat. Their food looked so delicious and expensive. They had all sorts of rich pastry, wine, huge grapes etc. We had to leave early and rush to make it

back for prep.

Nicole wrote a love story. She says it's fiction, but it's actually about her and Wei Keong (Sec 2 guy she likes). People have been teasing Nicole with Wei Keong since last year 'coz Nicole likes him but she denies it. Nicole thinks that Wei Keong likes her. Everything was revealed in the story, which she says has nothing to do with Wei Keong. She used the name Sally for the protagonist, but occasionally she used the word "I" instead of "she" for Sally. At the end of the story, Wei Keong asks her out, they become a couple, and they tell each other that they've been in love with each other since Sec 1! From the story, we know how highly she thinks of herself. She said that guys always give her their attention, and that all the guys are drawn to her, especially Sec 1 guys (Leo and friends). In the story, Wei Keong is jealous of her many admirers and loves her but dares not show it. She's so *perasan*!

The assistant manager of this hostel is Ms Lily Sim. She's a bitch. We call her Ass-man (short for assistant manager). She thinks she's very shapely and sexy, and she puts on lots of makeup. She goes around wearing fashionable minis and white stockings. She keeps catching Jen Nee and me. She's the one who gave Jen Nee the conduct form. Recently she keeps knocking at your door if you have guests after 11 pm. I always happen to be in that person's room when she knocks! She recognizes Jen Nee, Nancy and I and loves to see us get into trouble. We're going to play tricks on her. She knows we're out if our slippers, which she recognizes, are not at our door, so we must bring them in. Then she'll be running up and down in Block A looking for us. Or, we put all our slippers outside my door. Then she'll come to my door, go "knock, knock," and come into the room. Seeing no one but me, she'll ask everyone to "come out," thinking they're all hiding in the toilet. No one will come out. She'll go open the toilet door and Nicole will be inside, with a towel wrapped around her body. Then she'll open the wardrobe door where we'll have a mechanism that will spring out and punch her face! HA HA HA.

Tonight, we set a trap for Ass-Man by placing six pairs of slippers outside my door but unfortunately, she did not come.

Sunny's mind is very gross. She told us to apply anti-perspirant to our faces so all the sweat would clog up. Then, when you wash your face, all the sweat will gush out.

I noticed that many people here are freethinkers. And many ASEAN scholars have not pierced their ears and a lot of them wear contact lenses.

There's a Japanese student here for a few weeks in 3S1. In Singapore, if you study French or Japanese as a second language, and if you're good at it, they give you a free trip to France or Japan. There are a lot of opportunities if you study in Singapore and you're good at something.

Tuition teachers here earn so much. I heard a girl say that her Maths tuition is S$50 an hour and that the teacher seldom gives any work, just explains a bit! I can't stand it when people earn a lot without doing much.
Love, Pei Yi

Thursday 6 August

Dearest Mei Yee
I wish you were here 'coz there are many things that can't be written in letters, eg jokes, conversations, talking about people, going shopping together and having fun.

Yesterday I slept at three something 'coz I had to finish colouring My Heritage. I drew food and hawker centres. My figures have the same faces, look like rigid dummies and are so stiff. Ha! Ha!

Do you feel selfish, like you don't want to share your knowledge with others? I don't know why I'm like that sometimes. I'm trying to get rid of this attitude. For example, if you were here and I just finished reading *Cezanne* or *Women Who Changed History*, I'd probably tell you this and that. But I seldom do that to Jen Nee 'coz she's always asking for this and that and never really puts any effort to do anything herself. But I guess I'm being selfish for even having thoughts like "Should I share?" so I must change.

Mrs Jean just patted me on the back and said, "This one is working so hard," 'coz she thinks I'm studying History when I'm actually writing to you. Ha! Ha!

Oh my social life is so deprived! It's not even as good as yours although you don't live in a hostel. I love using this ink pen (which I found). Reply soon.
Love, Pei Yi

Friday 7 August

Dear Mei Yee
Today, there was National Day celebration in my school.

After that, I went to watch *My Cousin Vinny*, a comedy, with Lingling. Ralph Macchio (do you know who he is?) is so, so, so, so cute in that show. But he wasn't the main actor. His face is so cute, his lips look so kissable. He has the nicest lips I've ever seen. His nose is cute too.

Last night, Jen Nee and I missed prep 'coz we were too lazy to go. The Ass-man is so unreasonable. I hate that bitch. When I said I had a headache (my excuse for skipping prep) she said, "Talk too much, is it?" Then at 11 pm, she came knocking on my door. Jen Nee was with me and the bitch said, "If sick, why in her room?! Why after 11, still painting?!" She is so unreasonable. I HATE HER SO MUCH.

Well, bye.
Pei Yi

Friday 7 August

Dear Mei Yee

Hi! I've just posted you the latest letter, and am starting on another one now! I'm in love (and in lust) with Ralph Macchio! Just now, I was really crazy and "panting" for him in front of Elizabeth and Jen Nee. I said I want to kiss him, "Muaks! Muaks!" He is so cute!!! But 200% unattainable. Sigh. Jen Nee said looks are deceiving 'coz the first impression I give people is I'm a studious and quiet girl and she'd never imagine that I'm like this. Betty said I'm such a "deep" person because I listen to classical music, play chess, read books like *How to Begin to Study Literature*, *Beginner's Guide to Winning Chess* and books on Gandhi and Nehru.

Love, Pei Yi

Saturday 8 August

Dear Mei Yee

Hi! I just came back from a fun and exciting outing with Yoonphaik's church group. We went repelling: we climbed up a "mountain" (about five stories high) then we slid down using a rope:

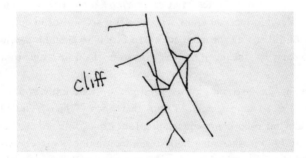

It was quite scary at first but a great experience! The people there were very nice, friendly and fun. They were very encouraging too. Jen Nee came with me too. We were so happy to have experienced this and to have made new friends. Next week, we're going to Sentosa Island with them.

Right now, Nancy's playing chess with me and she always ponders and ponders EVERY MOVE so I'm writing to you.
Love, Pei Yi

Sunday 9 August

Dear Mei Yee
National Day, so no school tomorrow. Yippee! The National Day celebrations in school on Friday would have filled my heart with patriotism if I were a Singaporean. There was a Mass. Our school, being a Holy Convent, is always having boring Masses. What a waste of time. There was also a concert. Two girls played two songs, which they composed themselves, on electric guitars.

I was thinking, if you were here, I probably wouldn't get close to Jen Nee. And if Jen Nee weren't here, I'd be close to someone else. Which goes to show it all depends on fate. Like, if there was a guy that would just hit it off with you, but if he already had a girlfriend, then both of you would never know what might have been.

Isn't it weird, if you've never seen something you just can't imagine but after seeing, you can. I mean, just a few seconds before I reached the place where we repelled, I didn't have any idea what it would be like. But now I do. Now you don't know what, let's say, Mrs Simons, looks like, but if you just see her for a few seconds, you would know.

Do you think looks are very important in a relationship? I think they are. Let's say Alisa had gone repelling yesterday. With her looks and charm, she'd probably have had guys falling all over themselves to help her. She's someone who can flirt without appearing like she's flirting. That's why the Sec 4 girls think she's so un-*hiau*.

I have high expectations in a boyfriend. He must have an intellectual,

119

intelligent mind, speak good English, like classical music (or at least know it)—you know what kind of person I mean, don't you? I hope I will find someone who likes me SOMEDAY. I told Jen Nee and she said the place to search for this kind of person is our hostel. Our hostel is full of people with a lot of potential.

Last night I played chess with Elizabeth for three hours! It was so fun. She moves without having a real plan sometimes but that move can sometimes "check" me or put herself in a very strategic position without her knowing it would! I play too impulsively. I must think harder for the competition. I find that I am very lazy. Let me rephrase. My body is quite hardworking but my mind is very lazy. In chess, I'm too lazy to think further than two moves.

Yesterday I tricked Ass-man. I put many, many pairs of slippers outside Jen Nee's door but Jen Nee was in my room. Ass-man knocked and knocked and shouted, "Warden!" while Jen Nee, Nancy and Elizabeth were actually in my room.
Love, Pei Yi

Tuesday 11 August

Dear Mei Yee
On Sunday (National Day) I went to watch *The Hand That Rocks The Cradle* with Jen Nee, Elizabeth and Sunny. It was a very good movie. It makes you feel very *geram* at first 'coz you know that Peyton is evil but the people in the movie don't. The plot and the planning are very clever.

After the movie, we went to have late supper, and then realized with a fright that it was way past the curfew so we rushed back to the hostel. We got to the hostel at midnight, and the gate was locked. So we started to crawl and slide under it, but when all of us except Sunny were inside already, and Sunny was right under the gate, Ms Lily Sim came out of the office and saw us standing by the gate. "What are you girls doing there at midnight!?" she screamed. We quickly stood right in front of

Sunny, who was still lying on the ground, so that Ms Lily Sim would not see her, and replied, "We're just walking around the hostel." She said, "Go back to your rooms! You're making too much noise!" Then, thank goodness, she walked away, so we quickly pulled Sunny up and then we all rushed back! What an adventure!

Oh Mei Yee … nothing … I think you understand my feelings about guys the most. I think I get crushes easily. I mean, so *kolot*. Talk a bit, then like already. I wish Eric and I were really friends, not acquaintances, and I wish he'd like me.

Glossary

kolot *Malay* backward in thinking, old-fashioned, especially in relationship matters

---

Today, I got myself into a hideous muddle that I now can't get out of. I'm so frustrated with myself. I didn't bring my lino cut for AEP 'coz I thought I had left it in school. Mr Como was quite displeased and he told me to stay back tomorrow and do it. I had to say yes. Then I realized tomorrow from 2 to 3.30 pm I have the chess tournament, which I've been spending hours and hours and hours practising for. Also tomorrow is audition day for school singers! I'm DEAD. Actually I also have violin lessons but I cancelled it just now. Aargh.

I feel so terrible 'coz:

1 I've so many things to tell you but I can't
2 I wish you were here to talk about Eric
3 I've so many things to do
4 The stupid muddle

I keep wasting time. Better say bye. I feel so *geram* that I've so many feelings that I can't tell you. Either can't write, forgot, or too trivial to write. BYE.

Love, Pei Yi

Wednesday 12 August

Dear Mei Yee
I kept worrying about today but it did not turn out that bad. Or that good either.

Today I rushed everywhere at school. I went to audition for school singers and I was so nervous that I forgot how to start singing. Mrs Loh was very kind though and let me have another audition next week. Jen Nee failed the audition 'coz she forgot the words.

At 2 pm sharp, I rushed to the classroom for chess and I had to play with Nancy and I lost! Losing to Nancy is extremely frustrating 'coz I usually beat her in the games we play. There was this timer which you have to press when you make a move. If your time runs out first, you lose. I was so nervous and panicky about the time that I did not even think. I just rushed headlong into disaster. The second round, I played with a girl from 3A1 and luckily I won. Next week, I can still play two more rounds. Oh, I wish I could play all over again. Then I'll think properly.

After chess, I rushed to the AEP room. Mr Como was not around until a few minutes after I got there, so luckily he didn't know that I was not there on time. Phew!

Do you think it's important to have intellectual classmates? I wish that I were in a better class. My class infuriates me, during Maths especially 'coz they'll waste the whole period arguing with Mr Koh. It's partly my fault—I was the one who told them what a bad Maths teacher he was. They don't know how bad their Maths is compared to students from other schools. Aargh. Also they have no initiative or interest to improve themselves or their studies. The 3S1 girls start doing their work once the teachers stop teaching and are as quiet as mice, while my class is as noisy as a fish market. I have the worst environment, facilities and opportunities of all the ASEAN scholars. I know we should be satisfied with what we have, make the best out of what we've got, and not compare and all,

but it just makes me so *geram*!
Pei Yi

Saturday 15 August

Dear Mei Yee
I wrote a story 'bout Ass-man. It was a funny story. I typed it out, then let people read. The funny thing was, Ass-man was just standing nearby when I was typing "Lily Sim woke up ..."

I hope I'll get a book published in this lifetime.

Last night, I was reading newspapers in the lounge and Eric was also there reading newspapers. Later, Alisa, Nancy and Jen Nee arrived as well so we all talked and Eric joined us. Then Sunny came and dominated the whole conversation and was funny, amusing and interesting.

Alisa is getting on my nerves 'coz she's SO pretentious and everyone sees the outer image she so successfully projects. Today, this girl from CHIJ was telling me that Alisa's an all-rounder—beautiful, smart, friendly, nice and athletic.

If you were here, I'd be telling you these things 'coz they're the sort of the things that are on my mind and bothering me:

1 Last night, everyone was being pretentious while talking to Eric and that I didn't really feel "in" the conversation once Sunny dominated it.
2 I'm bothered about my class 'coz I don't really fit in and also Jen Nee's classmates are a lot smarter. You know what I mean, don't you? My classmates are so shallow—they're not interested in anything, conversations with them are boring and you can't learn anything from them.
3 I'd tell you ALL the jokes I've heard.
4 I like Eric and feel terrible that we're not really friends.

Jen Nee said that I look like I am very comfortable talking and mixing with guys (which is not true). She said I can socialize and talk to so many people but I feel she is the one who gets along so well with everyone.

It's 2.40 am on Sunday. BYE.
Love, Pei Yi

Monday 17 August

Dear Mei Yee

It's prep time now. I feel so, so, so bad and embarrassed about something that just happened an hour ago, before dinnertime. It's so bad that I'm even embarrassed writing about it to you now. I just realized how bad it is to gossip and talk bad about someone. This is what happened: Sunny, Jen Nee and I were in the prep room before dinnertime, and we were talking about Nicole and laughing about her bad points. We thought that we were alone in the prep room because earlier we had checked the aisles between the rows of hutches, and also didn't hear anyone else there. Actually we didn't really plan to talk bad about Nicole. We were just talking about everyone in the hostel, who's dating who and stuff like that and the subject just went on to Nicole. Jen Nee and I totally forgot that a few months ago, we had resolved not to talk bad about people anymore. The bad things that we said about her were:

1 She's very *perasan* and thinks that all the guys like her
2 She is rather plump but thinks she's so slim. I told Sunny about how Nicole weighed 67 kg but blamed it on her shoes
3 She always talks in a *manja* voice to guys
4 She always talks about herself
5 She is irritating

Then, suddenly, we heard someone move from one of the rows near the door and leave the room. As that person walked past the windows of the prep room, we caught a glimpse of … Nicole!!! We felt so guilty, sorry and bad. Sunny, Jen Nee and I skipped dinner to look for her around the hostel but we couldn't find her. She also skipped prep. I feel so, so, so bad. What if she does something stupid like commit suicide?

It's eleven o'clock now After prep, Sunny, Jen Nee and I went to my room again to look for Nicole, and thank goodness she was there. She had been crying. We apologized profusely to her and tried to explain that we were just talking bad about many people and exaggerating to be funny. Basically we didn't have any good excuses, of course. She accepted our apologies. She said that she's aware that many people dislike her and we're the few friends that she has. That made us feel even worse. Mei Yee, I'm never going to bad-mouth anyone again. It's so mean, and really can really hurt someone. Even if they don't find out, it's still bad. Love, Pei Yi

Wednesday 19 August

Dear Mei Yee

Hi! It's now Malay period and we're doing a test. I'm so sleepy. On Sunday, Jen Nee and I went to Yoonphaik's Sunday School. There were two people there who talked to Jen Nee and me 'coz we were too new to join the others. They answered some of the questions we asked. I've decided that I don't want to go to Sunday School anymore 'coz I think I'll never be a Christian and I'll be wasting their time telling me about Jesus.

They said that Jesus is the only way to heaven. And ALL of us are sinners—we can never live up to God's expectations 'coz we're humans. And that makes us sinners? It was God who set those unattainable standards in the first place. They said that the first humans (Adam and Eve) were perfect until Adam ate an apple, thus committing a sin. So all men now have to die because of the sin. But because He loves us, He has given us a way to live eternally again—by believing and loving Jesus. Jesus sacrificed His life for us.

I feel that I would be fake and insincere if I were to suddenly believe in

Jesus and become a Christian. It's as though I only became a Christian 'coz I'm afraid to go to hell. Christians think that all those other people with other religions will perish in hell. That doesn't make sense at all to me. There are billions of people in this world who aren't Christian.

Also, they said, 'coz God loves us so much, he will keep trying to reach out to us and send people to tell us about him. In other words, Yoonphaik introducing Christianity to me is God's way of reaching out to me. Yoonphaik asked us to go to Sunday School and Jen Nee said we should go at least once since we only join them for fun activities.

So I suppose I'm all to blame for not becoming Christian since God has reached out to me. He's probably thinking, "That silly stubborn girl, blah, blah, blah." Don't get me wrong, it's not that I do not believe there's a God, it's just that I can't be committed heart and soul to Jesus, have total faith, and trust in Him like Christians do. In fact, I find the way they talk scarry. I wouldn't want to be like that. Jen Nee thinks it's good for them to believe and it doesn't matter if it's true as long as it makes them do good things. But I can't accept that. I will only accept something if it's true regardless of the results.

And what's that about being saved, as if we're now living a tortured, terrible life? If another person tells me that I sin, I'm going to freak out. Thank goodness, the people in that church are really nice and friendly, and they don't preach and pressurize you into converting. So I don't really feel so terrible. But right after Sunday School, I was feeling pretty bothered about everything.

Do you have this "movie" in your mind of "The Perfect Life"? I do— often. It's clearly playing in my mind and it goes like this: You and I came to Singapore together, we're roommates, I'm in a Science class with some ASEAN scholars, we work hard 'coz there's competition, life's so meaningful etc. I should stop thinking 'bout it and comparing it with my present life. I want to develop a strong personality and be confident and know myself well and be "whole". Today, the schools in Singapore were ranked. In first place was RI, second was RGS (they're so lucky). Our school ranked so low—fourteenth or fifteenth. Nanyang is sixth or seventh.

Nicole and I did this set of questions for a survey. She pretended it was for her library project and handed out ten copies to Eric, Cheng Hoe, Matt, Elizabeth, Alisa and some others. I was dying to read Eric's answers. I find that they're all very mature and they care more about studies than BGR (boy-girl-relationships) or popularity. They're mostly confident people with goals who find life meaningful. The first question "Do you always keep striving in life?" was unanimously answered "yes". I've decided to forget 'bout boys. Reading their answers made me feel so silly and shallow.

Alisa (who's very hardworking) doesn't even think of guys. She has many admirers though. A guy from another hostel dedicated a song to her on the radio. Right now, I feel that everyone else's life is more meaningful than mine because they have a goal to work towards. When I don't have a goal, I feel empty and depressed and right now, I don't have one, really. I'm going to change—no more guys, guys, guys.

I want to show you what they wrote in the survey:

Question #1: Do you feel you have to keep striving for more and more in life?
All ten answered "Yes".

Question #2: How do you feel about girls making the first move?
Eric: It implies that they are confident and not strapped down by the cumbersome moral values of the ancient. I don't object to it at all.
Leo: I do not wish to indulge in such cases.

Question #3: What do you think about BGR at your age?
Eric: It's permissible only if it doesn't interfere with my other priorities, namely my academic performance.
Leo: Extremely terrible and disgusting.

Question #4: Do you feel that your life is meaningful now? Please elaborate.

Eric: Only if I don't think about the bad side of things! It depresses me very much if I do. I try to look for the light at the tunnel, the silver lining etc adinfinitum, to retain my sanity.

Elizabeth: Yup! Studies are OK, social life is OK, money situation is OK, ECA is OK and—finally found a goal to work towards. Life is beautiful.

(All ten of them answered that they have a meaningful life.)

Question: #5 What do you think of one-night stands?

Cheng Hoe: Very good, if they will be infected with AIDS or STD after that (preferably AIDS).

Question #6: Do you feel it is a "must" to socialize? Please elaborate.

Eric: Only if you really enjoy it and you do not disgust anyone! I suppose you gotta have friends to help U along the way.

Cheng Hoe: Who said so? Robinson Crusoe could survive alone, why can't we?

Question #7: Do you feel it is important to be popular?

Eric: No. The cliché "be yourself " and all that corny stuff still works. I don't care or need to be popular.

Cheng Hoe: Let it come naturally. If you always strive to be popular, it will get even further from you.

Question #8: At what age do you think we should start dating?

Eric: At the fateful age when Cupid is up to mischief again and starts firing arrows … with a machine gun. 13–15 years old=group dates; 16 years old=tadaa!!; 18 years old=get a tux, order a corsage, grab that cologne!

Question #9: What qualities do you find attractive in the opposite sex?

Eric: Confidence in oneself and sophistication in personality, not forgetting, OF COURSE, sugar and spice and everything nice—oh yeah, most important, maturity in thinking!

Cheng Hoe: Innocent, industrious.

Matt: A strong, powerful character.

Question #10: What is the ideal personality in your future partner?

Eric: Err ... ahem ... cough, cough ... can I skip this? Just kidding, OK? Well, I'd like her to be sophisticated, sensitive, understanding, caring, humorous and liked by most people.

Cheng Hoe: She should possess the same interests and personalities as mine.

Matt: A character that is frank and direct. A firm grip on emotions, so won't crack easily.

Leo: I do not wish to have a partner!

Leo's answers are so funny that I laughed till I had a stomachache. For all the questions about girls, he put "I do not want a future partner/I do not think about it and have no opinions." He must be gay or is destined for priesthood. When asked to list according to priorities "friends, money, career, love life, family" he put "family, religion ..." and didn't put love life at all!

Love, Pei Yi

Friday 21 August (*Class trip to Malacca!!*)

Dear Mei Yee

Hi! Guess where I am. I'm now in Room 701 of City Bayview in Malacca. This morning, at 7 am, we started our journey to Malacca. My classmates are so fascinated with the souvenirs and key chains made of wood on which the sellers write their names. They spent a ton on junk. Lingling spent RM154.20! I spent less than RM10. They were also surprised at the narrow streets. I'm sharing the room with Huiwee, Lingling and Yoonphaik. We've visited some historical sites like the Dutch Square, Hang Li Poh's well and A Famosa. Have you been to Malacca before?

Love, Pei Yi

Saturday 22 August

Dear Mei Yee

I saw your letter when I reached the hostel this evening. In the bus today while I was sleeping, I dreamed that I received your letter and then when I came back, I really did.

The tour had been educational but I also learned something about myself. I realized that I've been acting like a spoilt brat sometimes (not all the time) 'coz I want my own way and everyone is so nice to me, nicer than I am to them. So I'm going to change and stop being spoilt.

Love, Pei Yi

Friday 28 August

Dear Mei Yee

I have so many things to tell you. Let me do it in chronological order.

On Tuesday, Nicole told me that she had a confession to make—that she lied when she said those guys asked her to dance at the campfire she attended. She said she can't help lying sometimes—it just comes out of her mouth without her realizing, then she realizes later and but it's too late. It sounded so preposterous and I couldn't really believe such a thing could happen but when I told Jen Nee, she said it's true—she read in the newspapers that it's a sort of a disease— you lie without being aware of it! Gosh, poor Nicole! I hope she can change.

Sister Elaine, the headmistress, had a talk with Sec 3 ASEAN scholars in my school. She talked incessantly in a monologue for one whole hour. I found that quite amazing. She talked about scholars needing to behave exemplarily. Then she said Nicole, my roommate, who's in Sec 2 so she wasn't at the talk, has been doing quite badly in exams. Nicole had been given talks by MOE people and Sister Elaine, asking her if she had any problems. I doubt that Nicole will have her scholarship renewed if she doesn't improve. She doesn't really seem to study or care. Then today, she told Jen Nee and I that she has been under too much pressure, especially from her dominating and demanding mother. Her mother has placed really high hopes on Nicole and wants her to excel and fulfill her mother's dreams. According to Nicole, her mother is really pressurizing and unreasonable but I don't know if she was just trying to justify her laziness.

Jen Nee and I tried to give her advice and motivate her to study. Then we wanted to call Teensline together with her to get more advice from the counsellors, as they may have better advice, because we didn't really know how to help her but the phone line was engaged for a long time. So many people have problems!

Nicole is also not getting along with her Batchlings. By the way, there is no such word as Batchlings, I think. They find her irritating. Nicole told us that they always leave her out so we try to help her by giving her advice like 1) listen to people when they talk, 2) stop talking 'bout herself. But Nicole is really weird. She started talking about herself almost at once and her long, boring monologue is such a put-off. We tried to help her but she doesn't seem to be able to change!

Jen Nee and I decided that we will include Nicole more in our social activities, like invite her to go out to lunch and movies with us on weekends.

On Wednesday we had a rehearsal for Mid-Autumn Festival where I would be singing. I was feeling terrible 'coz at the rehearsal, I was so nervous that I couldn't sing properly. The reason for my fear was the Sec 3 guys were there, we were all in an enclosed room and I was in a terrible giggling fit during our singing. Eric was there—that made everything worse. Sophisticated, matured, confident?? I was giving the impression of being a silly, giggling idiot. That is something that I want to eradicate from my personality. No more giggling! Anyway I spent two days feeling bothered 'bout it. Nicole was also so nervous at the rehearsal that her lips were quivering.

On Thursday, the Mid-Autumn Festival was great! Immensely enjoyable—with scrumptious cuisine and hilarious performances. One sketch, acted by Matt, Cheng Hoe and Gaik Teong, was entitled "Life". Cheng Hoe's rap was "Life ... can only be meaningful with knowledge" and we laughed and laughed 'coz he's a hardworking intellectual (a mugger toad). We were roaring with laughter. My *langit langit* (the top of my mouth) hurt from laughing. The other sketch was even funnier—about hostel life. Gaik Teong was the cook and when he was frying, he dug "gold" in his nostrils, picked lice from his hair, scratched all over, and then it all went into the food! He was such a good actor and the whole thing was SO funny. The last item was our song "The Sound of Music" which has three parts. This time it was not a flop like the rehearsal because I was determined to sing confidently.

Guess what? I'm pregnant. Ha! Ha! No, lah. Actually, I wanted to say I can swim freestyle already. Not really good but at least I can get from one end of the pool to the other (not the length of the pool, though, just the width).

At the Mid-Autumn Festival, there was a quiz. One of the questions was "What is the distance between the earth and the moon?" We were thinking, how do we know. Then Cheng Hoe answered: "385,000 km" and it was correct!! Typical Cheng Hoe! Ha! Ha! There were prices for the quiz and lucky draws. Each performing group received S$30. There was this question in the quiz "What year did Apollo land on the moon?" and I raised my hand but the warden did not see. Those who answered were wrong, then he went on to another question. (Is it 1976?) I'm still in the "keep striving for more" mood. Hope it lasts.

Eric is very popular with the Networking Club members in my school. He's popular with everyone, in fact. I think it's because when he talks to you, he does so properly, like he's giving you his full attention, and he also projects a VERY good image—confident, knowledgeable, interesting, funny and cute.

I can just imagine how much Nancy will love you if you're here 'coz she'll be SO impressed with your piano playing. Mine's terrible and she's impressed. She'll jack you. She's very good at jacking people.

Glossary
jack to jack someone is to suck up to someone

I was given a list to choose from for my AEP O level project: architecture, sculpture, landscaping, photography (requires extra expenses), stained glass (also expensive), ceramics (boring), costume, jewellery, etc. I want something adventurous and challenging that is outdoors, and not something where I'll be sitting in a room trying to think what to do. I still do not know what to do. I want to stay here for JC (Junior College), I think.

Isn't it funny—in the future, everyone we know will be married and have a profession? Well, good night (although it might not be night when you're reading this).
Love, Pei Yi (The Now-Keeps-Wanting-To-Improve)

Thursday 3 September

Dear Mei Yee
Hi!

Nancy showed me a book entitled *The Unexplained*. Some Christians and popes exhibit signs of Jesus' crucifixion! They may have scars on their hands where Jesus was nailed, some bleed from their head!!

I think it's so silly of me to "save a minute and waste an hour". To save time, last night I wrote one short paragraph in the toilet. Later, however, I wasted two hours reading a trashy romance book. After that, I wished I'd used those two hours more wisely.

Tuesday was a holiday 'coz it was Teachers' Day. Just now, we watched *Weekend Reunion*—a movie from the Archie comics about what happened when all of them met 15 years after graduation. Archie is engaged to a new girl, Veronica has divorced four times, Betty has a bully as a boyfriend. Very, very funny.

Oh ya, I just found out that Apollo landed on the moon in 1969 so it's a good thing that the people did not ask me to answer when I raised my hand.

I'm always feeling bothered. It's very bad and it's 'coz it's sort of my habit and I just always subconsciously succeed in finding something to be bothered about. Very bad. I must stop thinking of things that could have been. I'm always thinking, "If I'd been in 3S1, I might have found someone who could discuss things that are interesting"; "If I'd been in 3S1, I could ask Mr Tan. And he'd teach very well. The way he solved the questions is very good. I wouldn't be having problems in class." In fact I think everyone except me looks like they have no problems. Never mind. I must forget my problems concerning my class and just think that someday the problems won't be there anymore. It's pretty weird, things that seem to be a big problem to you at one time can seem so trivial when you look back at it next time.

For the whole of this month, there's a "Speak Mandarin Campaign". Everyday, there'll be a simple conversation written in the newspapers and you can call toll-free to listen to a recorded conversation to teach you. I'm going to call daily. Huiwee's teaching me some Chinese. I wish I was learning Chinese instead of Malay 'coz every Malay period's just a waste of time. No improvement, instead I'm deteriorating.

Next week is one-week hols! Yippee!!! Tomorrow is the last day of school for the term.

I was joking when I wrote that I want to take a cooking course—maybe, if I cook really delicious dishes for Eric's mother, she will force him to marry me!
I'm really looking forward to the holidays. I'm going to start studying for

the exams. Is it amazing to start a month ahead? Everyone here is constantly studying, improving and becoming cleverer and cleverer, so it's not amazing to start studying so soon. Final exams are three weeks after school reopens. Remember you once said, "What's the use of being clever?" I think life is only meaningful with knowledge. I think if you were to come to Singapore, you'd do very well.

Well, BYE.
Love, Pei Yi

Friday 11 September
Dear Mei Yee
Hi! It's now 3 am. No, I just checked the clock—it's 5.10 am on Friday. The reason I did not sleep last night was we went to the Educational Night Tour. Oh no, holidays are coming to an end—I enjoyed myself tremendously and I still have a lot of things to do and study.

Let me start from where I last stopped writing. Elizabeth, Nicole, Jen Nee and I went to Omnimax to watch a 3D show. It was *The Great Barrier Reef* (in Australia) and it cost an exorbitant S$10!

Today there were Caucasians playing rugby at the hostel field and Jen Nee was so excited 'coz she thinks Caucasians are cute.

Now about the Educational Night Tour—first, we had supper at a place called Lau Pa Sat where there are food stalls. S$3 for a plate of fried *kuay teow*. Then we played some games and walked around West Coast Park, where many couples seem to enjoy the seaview in the dark. By the way, this tour is free and it's very educational. Two male wardens who're very fun and nice went with us and Ms Lily Sim (Ass-man) came too. She flirted with the JC guys. The only Sec 3 guys were Matt, Cheng Hoe and Eric. I think Matt is self-centered and wants to control everything. At Lau Pa Sat while having supper, we played Truth or Dare—we turn a straw on the table and if you're picked, you have to answer any question the person at the other end of the straw asks. When Jen Nee asked Cheng

Hoe which girl in the hostel he fantasizes about, he said, "No one" and that's the truth. Matt says he has never talked about girls. He just doesn't! Weirdo. Luckily I wasn't picked 'coz if they ask me about liking someone, I'd have to say "Eric" or do something they dare me to.

Then we went to an abattoir—where pigs are slaughtered. It was a very enlightening, emotional and horrifying experience. The worst thing about the abattoir was the hair-raising wails and screams of the pigs. When the pigs were in the pen, about to be electrocuted to make them unconscious, they knew they were going to die. The screams could be heard even from the pen outside the abattoir. At first I thought it was the noise of machinery! They had to be forced and beaten to go to be electrocuted. Then their throats were slit but they looked as if they're still struggling, even with their legs hanging up. The red blood gushed out like a tap turned on full force. The pigs looked like they were choking on their own blood.

We saw many, many pigs, one after another, like they were toys in a factory line. The pigs went into a machine where jets of boiling water removed their hairs. Then they went through a fire that burns away fine hairs. Many workers along the machine line cut up their carcasses and their organs to be sold. There are hundreds and hundreds of pigs slaughtered every night!

The air was filled with the pungent stench of pig blood. I held my nose throughout the whole thing but most people could stand it. It's totally terrible to work here. I feel sorry for all the workers. The man cutting the throats waved at us.

After watching all that, we went outside. Some nice workers answered our questions. They get S$60 a night—they're from Malaysia 'coz Singaporeans do not want this terrible job.

Then we went to the pen which really stunk of shit and all the smelliest things. I was horrified to see the pigs being forced into the abattoir where they would be electrocuted. They were struggling and wailing in desperation while being whacked and pushed into a death sentence for a crime they did not commit. Actually, they looked quite cute. I looked at one and the eyes looked so sad that I started crying. It was very embarrassing. Luckily it was quite dark and only a few people knew. I've decided not to eat pork for the rest of my life. I know killing chicken or fish or ants is just the same—they all have lives—but I just can't eat pork anymore.

The eerie thing 'bout the pigs' screams was that it sounded human-like—like women screaming as they're being tortured.

Everyone was excited about going to Bugis Street during the Night Tour 'coz there're supposed to be many transvestites there but we just passed by (did not alight for safety reasons) and we did not see a single transvestite. Or many we couldn't tell from their appearance.

I've so much to prepare for Final Exams. I haven't done much work during the hols. I'm reading *The History of Art*. All the way from cave paintings to Sumerian to Greek to Roman to Modern Art.

Sometimes I wish I was a good flirt and sometimes I don't care. I think it's better to care 'bout studies first—like Eric does. But then, every girl either has a very good impression of him or likes him.

Sunday 12 September

Dear Mei Yee

Today is the last day of holiday—Sunday 12/9!! I wish I can stop time. I still haven't received your letter!! Did you receive mine—the one with Eric's answers to the survey??

Friday was Mid-Autumn Festival so we carried lanterns and walked around the hostel at night.

Then we watched *Mary Lou Prom Night II* on TV. Did you watch *Irreconcilable Differences*? I think it's on Malaysian TV. Very funny.

Yesterday, Jen Nee and I went to Yoonphaik's church to watch a video 'bout satanism in pop music. The songs the heavy-metal groups sing are terrible. They advocate free sex, satanism, drug abuse, violence and suicide. Their songs have caused many teenagers to commit torture killings. USA is such a wild country. The pictures of their CDs are horrible—terrifying skulls, monsters, devils and signs of satanism.

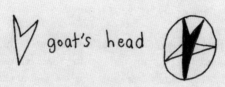

They draw really devilish and diabolical stuff such as a goat's head inside a star. Their lyrics read: "Suicide is a solution to problems. I can't stand my meaningless life anymore. I take a gun and put it in my mouth. Soon I will be free …" and "Slick and Slide. I push it in. Make love till you are blind." The dancing on stage is like making love, no, I mean having sex. They teach really bad values. I wonder why they want to do that. Anyway, I've never liked stupid noisy heavy metal. But those groups have tons of fans and sometimes they go so wild that they kill each other during concerts. I saw this concert where the rock star cut his own arm with a sword and drank cups of blood! Axl Rose of Guns and Roses has a ring on his nipple!! Samantha Fox, Bananarama, George Michael, Bobby Brown, Elvis Presley and the Beatles are among the worst groups.

I just LOVE children's storybooks. I read a few at a rent-a-book bookstore at Coro. So cute! I love the illustrations. The plot is cute and the characters are cute. There's one 'bout a group of farm animals. This sheep is very silly. When all the animals sit down to think of an idea, they all have "thought bubbles" above their heads but the sheep's bubble is empty! Ha! Ha! Ha!

BYE. PLEASE REPLY SOON!
Love, Pei Yi

Tuesday 14 September

Dearest Mei Yee
Hi! I'm so happy to receive your letter—at last!

Congrats for getting a Merit for Quartet. Why do you say your social life is zero? I think it's OK 'coz you mix with Jackson and orchestra people. Actually in class, Huiwee is my only good friend. But I'm not bothered and I don't regret going to my class anymore. I guess I learned from my feeling-bothered-about-my-class times and have managed to adapt.

Mei Yee, please don't worry that our friendship won't be close anymore! Just because my best friend in Singapore is Jen Nee doesn't mean that you and me aren't best friends for life! We will always be best friends. Also, I can tell you some things that I can't tell Jen Nee. I think it's because she's here that there is a little bit of competitiveness between us, even though it's not out in the open. Just a little bit. Like I will be a little jealous if she does better than me overall. Please, please, please come to JC in Singapore a year from now. Then you, me and Jen Nee will have so much fun!

About Eric … I'm in love with him but as usual all the guys I like do not like me. I must try to talk to Eric more, like when I see him reading newspapers. The trouble is I do not know what to talk to him about. Oh ya, Eric has good grooming and dressing sense, he always looks very clean and "put together" and he has a beautiful body. He also gives me the impression that he is very interesting and fun to be with. The long and short of it is that I'm head over heels in crush with him. I wish that he and I were good friends (since bf and gf seems too remote a possibility). Oh ya, I just remembered. When we were doing deco for Farewell and Eric was on his hands and knees, drawing on the huge paper on the floor, he looked so … so gorgeous. (His body, I mean.) Well, if you're disgusted … bye. Reply soon.

And how did you know I'll fall in love with Eric? Actually I guess I knew it too but I just didn't want to.
Love, Pei Yi

Wednesday 16 September (*Haven't eaten pork for six days*)

Dear Mei Yee
Guess what? I came forth in the chess competition! Yes! I'm so happy. At first I thought that only the winner would get a trophy but there're actually four trophies. Three of the top four winners were Malaysians, and one was Singaporean. Next year, I'm resigning from swimming, violin and choir and joining chess and LDDS (Literary, Drama and Debate Society). If I join chess, then I can go with them to all the competitions against other schools. Actually, I like Choir too but there're too few Choir members (only 20!) and we never do much, not even competitions or performances.

I read this really GREAT and funny story by Jeffrey Archer. He's my favorite author—I really admire his style. When you read his short story, you don't know where it's leading and at the end there's a twist, which is so ingenious and unexpected! Oh ya, the story was "Broken Routine" in the book *A Quiver Full of Arrows* (in case you want to read it).

Well, bye.
Love, Pei Yi

Sunday 20 September

Dear Mei Yee
I just received your letter today. How were your exams?

Today, I got back my Macbeth Lit. test. I'm so happy to get full marks. Lingling was the other one in my class to get 12/12. Lingling said I spread my motivation and drive to the people sitting around me.

Did you watch *City of Joy*? I didn't see it, but Jen Nee and Sunny told me the story. It's very (100x) touching and even more so because it shows the real conditions of the poor people in the slums of India. So sad. I wish I can do something to make a change but I can't. Their government should educate them and control the population.

I'm so horrified to know about the Serbs cutting up the pregnant woman!!! My God. How can they ever do such things?!

It's very heartbreaking that Eric doesn't like me so I shall not care about him anymore. We're not even friends. I'm always dumbfounded when he says something witty. Sunny and Jen Nee are quite witty. Yesterday, Nancy (who's very brave with guys) asked Eric to draw something and Jen Nee said, "This is your chance to talk to him" when Nancy went to his hutch in the prep room, so Jen Nee and I followed. Anyway, he hadn't drawn anything and we were just standing there. He said, "Is this a tourist attraction?" ('coz we were staring at him in his hutch) and I didn't know how to answer and I said yes (which is so stupid to say) and Jen Nee said, "Are you complimenting yourself?"

I'm so happy that you're applying for ASEAN scholarship!! Are you going to take Science in JC too?

The other day, Jen Nee and I played this very funny game of Creating A Play, or Consequences. The characters in our play are people from the hostel. Let's say you and your partner agree to write as Elizabeth and Matt. For example, you write, "Elizabeth: Oh Matt I'm so ugly. I wish I wasn't so fat." Then you fold the paper over and pass it to your partner. Maybe your partner (who doesn't know what you wrote) writes: "Yes. I agree." It was SO funny. We laughed and laughed.

Here's an example of what we wrote:

Play #1

Matt (written by Jen Nee): Cheng Hoe! Cheng Hoe! Let's go to the activities room and socialize.

Cheng Hoe (written by me): Matt, I have a secret to tell you. You know I never talk about girls. But actually I think about them ALL THE TIME! I don't want to look at my Physics books anymore. What shall I do?

Matt: So are you going to the activities room or not?

Cheng Hoe: No I don't want to do that. I want to have some fun. Let me tell you what happened last night. A Nanyang girl came up to me and said that she thinks you're ugly. I told her that she's right. Do you agree?

Matt: No.

Cheng Hoe: You idiot! Why did you say no. Didn't we agree on that earlier? Do you want to go to the disco. I want to ask Ms Lily Sim if she wants to go. Look, she's with that guy again—Niles.

Matt: Bullshit! You're talking rot. I think Niles likes me better.

Cheng Hoe: Oh, thank you for saying that. You always make me feel better, you know. One day I must repay you. What do you want me to do?

Matt: Ai yooi. Of course lah. You have so many pimples on your nose.

Cheng Hoe: Why you so cheap one?! Must *tiau keh* a bit what! I'm so ashamed of you. Hey look, Niles is coming. Ask him what he thinks.

Matt: OK, no problem. I think I can bear with the thought that Nicole likes you.

Glossary

tiau keh Hokkien literally means raise the price, a slang expression for playing hard to get

---

Play #2:

Pei Yi (written by Jen Nee): Oh Eric! Oh! Oh! Eriiiiic! I'm aching for you. Don't you want me. Say you do. We make a perfect couple.

Eric (written by me): I never knew. But I guess I have to tell you that I'm actually gay. What do you think can cure me. I'm the president of the Networking Club. If I'm not cured, I may get kicked out.

Pei Yi: Eric, let's go swimming. I'm yearning to see your body. The memory of you crawling around when we were doing the deco is still fresh in my mind.

Eric: What do you find so attractive about me? I never knew that people find me attractive. Alisa and our ex-classmates always say I'm Alvin the Chipmunk.

Pei Yi: Maybe. Maybe not. That depends on how you interpret it. Hey look, here comes those CHIJ Networking Club girls. Let's pretend we don't know them.

Eric: Let's do it then. I quite agree with you. Where do you want to go watch *City of Joy*?

Pei Yi: Please don't talk to them. They're so loud-mouthed and flirtatious. I'm sure you only like girls like me. You know I used to dream of you every night and used to moan and lament 'cause you weren't mine then.

Eric: Have you seen my Cow glue? I lost it. Oh no! It's in my pocket and it's all spilled. I'm glued to this spot on the ground now.

Pei Yi: Go away! I thought you were loyal to me but looks like you are a big flirt. You wanna know something. Alisa didn't tell me you look like Alvin the Chipmunk. I thought of it myself. Ha! Ha! Ha! Alvin the Chipmunk, Alvin the Chipmunk!.

Eric: I love you. I hope we'll get married someday.

Play #3:·

Alisa (written by me): Oh my back hurts from dancing and shaking so much last night! I need someone to massage it.

Gaik Teong (written by Jen Nee): Juliet, Juliet, where at thou Juliet. Show your pretty face to your Romeo and he shall protect you from the cruelty of humankind.

Alisa: Thank you. I feel so much better now. We should do this more often, you know. Gaik Teong, I hear that there's a girl in the hostel after you. I hope it's not true!

Gaik Teong: Come on darling, pretty please. Let me touch you. My hand is aching to touch you. It's aching so much that I have to apply Mopiko.

Alisa: Let's go swimming. I want you to see my new bikini. It's your fav colour and size: transparent and teeny.

Gaik Teong: Oh no. Not again. Why must we always go through this. I guess this is the consequence of dating a beautiful girl.

Alisa: No, I do not agree. I think that we make a a terrific couple. Let's get married once I finish my O levels! Please. I'm pregnant. Have you no feelings for your baby?

Gaik Teong: Yes! Of course yes. Yes, yes, yes, yes. I am yours; if only you'll say yes too. Eeek! What is that!? A frog, a frog! Alisa, save me!

Alisa: What! You want me to abort the child! You heartless, obscene, insensitive pig! I will marry Matt tomorrow and dump you!

Gaik Teong: How fortunate. If not for you, that frog would probably be jumping around here just now.

Yesterday, Nicole and I washed our very dirty toilet bowl. We were so disgusted. We held our noses and she brushed it. At last when all the soap powder was flushed away, we were rewarded with a white, shiny toilet. A far cry from the dark, brown, yellowish one a few minutes before that!

Glossary

Mopiko a brand of ointment for mosquito bites

I'm very ambitious about Final Exam. What I mean is, doing well counts a lot to me. I've sort of "overcome" feeling terrible 'bout being in a class of people-who-are-not-that-intellectual.

Cheng Hoe said all the guys are prepared for their Finals. The guys (ASEAN scholars) are either SO hardworking or SO ingenious.

Nicole is so stressed about Finals. She is studying very hard, which is good, but she kept getting depressed and having anxiety attacks. She says that she wants to get some pills that improve memory.

About Eric, I wish that he'll like me but as this is just one of my inaccessible dreams (like David Copperfield/Keng Joon/Larry/Li Ming/King Kong/Gary/Brad/Kirk Cameron/Ricky Schroeder), I shall stop thinking about him.

Love, Pei Yi

PS My recent monthly test results were not quite satisfying. No, I've not become a marks freak. These are my August marks:

English Composition: 27/40 (must at least get 30 for the finals)
English Comprehension: $29^1/2$/50 (so low!)
History: 16/20
Literature: 17/20
E.Math: 83/100 (so terrible! I should get full marks)
Add. Math: 34 1/2/40 (so terrible too! I should get full marks)
Chem: 28/37 (must do real well)
Physics: 34/40 (must do real well)
AEP: 69/100 (deplorable!)
Principle of Accounts: $43^1/2$/50 (must get full marks)

Saturday 26 September

Dear Mei Yee
Hi! I've so many things to tell you.

Yesterday, Elizabeth sort of gave me an English lesson. She's good at everything! Her English is really good. She got 30/30 for comprehension at the beginning of the year and the English teacher said she's never given anyone 30/30 before! Elizabeth wants to be an English teacher next time 'coz she wants to show people the beauty of English, so that they can learn to love it. Elizabeth has a classmate who is giving Primary 1 tuition and getting S$70 an hour (!) for one person. That girl just gives exercises from a workbook! Everyone here is very studies-oriented because they have GEP (Gifted Educational Programme) streaming and everyone wants to go in. There are only three schools with GEP classes: RGS, RI and ACS. GEP pupils get tons and tons of privileges! They get specially-trained teachers who teach them almost one-to-one, they have different time tables from the normal students, they do different worksheets, they get brought to Egypt and everywhere, they get EVERYTHING. There're only a few people per class. They find O levels *kacang putih*. At the beginning of the year, let's say a girl gets into GEP (just scraping through) and a girl misses by a few marks, after a year, they'll be miles apart! That is what I feel about the ASEAN scholars who get to go to RGS—they get all the best teachers, best facilities, environment, blah blah blah. It's unfair! Elizabeth is really good at everything. The English standard in her school is much higher than ours. Elizabeth can quote from memory passages from Julius Caesar.

Glossary

kacang putih Malay literally a collective name for a variety of nuts; a slang term used to imply that something is very easy

---

Anyway, last night Jen Nee and I were feeling quite bothered about all this. Which is why I really want to get into RJC (Raffles Junior College). To get into RJC, you need the minimum aggregate of six points and RGS and RI people automatically get two points. It's unfair. I feel that if we'd gone to RGS, our potential would've been developed much better. It's not as if we won't do as well as some of those ASEAN scholars who're in RGS. I feel it's unfair 'coz our potentials are not developed to the fullest. Just take English lessons. The English lessons I have aren't really beneficial but Elizabeth's teacher teaches them how to improve this and that and give them really interesting work. Elizabeth said she wants to go to university and just learn and learn and give lectures and talk to intellectual people and never graduate for her whole life. Oh ya, if you're the top person in GEP, you might as well consider yourself the smartest girl in Asia. I think in Malaysia, there are surely many more people cleverer than those in GEP, but they never get the opportunity to develop their potential and then it becomes lost. Oh, I just can't stand it. Anyway, I can't do anything 'bout it.

Love, Pei Yi

Monday 5 Octocber

Dear Mei Yee

Just received your letter. Let me answer your questions first.

Yes, you're right that I shouldn't always compare and complain about my class and how the Science classes have more opportunities than me. I do feel bad that I am not always thankful for my circumstances, which are not bad at all compared to many people. I actually already posted to you more letters where I again compared and complained about such things—please just ignore those parts. I actually constantly try not to complain. I make lists in my diary to convince myself that being in my class instead of a Science class is actually a blessing in disguise, but maybe I should just admit to myself that it was a irrevocable mistake and then just live with it. I mean, it's just two years of my life, and I still have so many years ahead of me. Sometimes when I think about it I feel so bad for wanting my classmates to be so intellectual. I mean, they're so nice to me and I'm just like a spoilt brat if I expect them to be so clever—they can't change.

Yes, Mid-Autumn Festival is Mooncake/Lantern/Zhong Qiu Jie Festival. I don't care 'bout guys now. The last guy I talked to was Gaik Teong—he's so funny. He's also very mean to Nancy. Let me start from the very beginning. Nancy was sitting on the prep room table, in the hutch, curled up so Jen Nee and I asked Gaik Teong to stand up and look. He said, "How can that thing fit into a hutch?!" I said, "Coz she's a rabbit." He said, "I don't see the resemblance." Then I asked him 'bout his lessons in school and I read his English worksheet to improve my English. Then I asked him why he is so mean to lead Nancy on, like giving her a rose during Farewell. He said, "She was looking so desperate and I had no one to give the rose to." I said, "We were all standing around and even more desperate, how come you didn't give us?!" He said, "I didn't know you were desperate. If not, I give you, loh."

I respect people who are naturally clever. I think all ASEAN scholars are very special—every one of them has a special quality if you look carefully. The Singapore government is so clever to get all the brains to work for Singapore. Did I tell you next time I want to live in Singapore? I just love it here.

I feel so happy to be one of the ASEAN scholars. Last Sat, we had a Sec 3 and Sec 4 Batch Outing to the Botanic Gardens where we sat and played games and Ekan played the guitar. So fun! We played this game with two teams. Nancy (the host, naturally—she loves being leader and is quite good at it) says, "Send out the person with the LONGEST LEGS or can talk the most nonsense without stopping!" Then, both teams compete. We sent Elizabeth for the person who can talk the most nonsense without stopping and she chattered away as fast as an MRT without a single break!

During the recent outing, Eric went but he didn't really participate. Instead, he just stood at the back and watched. He looks blur sometimes and he blinks his eyes as if he's confused.

The guys kept catching another guy then rolled him on the grass, pounced on him and opened his shirt then took a photo. How embarrassing. They did it to Eric too.

I feel so sad for the poor soldiers who died in WWI and WWII. I feel sad when I read about how their comrades tried to save them. The British really did a lot for Malaya, especially during the Emergency Period (1948–1960). Oh ya, the Malay word for the Emergency is *Darurat*—I couldn't recall the word for a second.

Glossary

Malaya the old name of Malaysia before it gained independence from the British in 1957

My Malay is crumbling away, rotting, deteriorating. I've only read one Malay book this year. Jen Nee has read none.

Sometimes I feel so grateful to my parents for giving me so much—their love and all their hopes for me.

Mei Yee, thank you for the years of our friendship. Hope you come to

Singapore for JC—there're so many things you'll like here. Meanwhile, enjoy yourself in BM. I find that if you cope with your problems wisely and look for the silver lining it's not that bad after all. Well, at the time I'm writing this letter, I'm in a happy mood—I might just become frustrated later on.

Well, BYE.
Love, Pei Yi

Saturday 18 October

Dear Mei Yee

I'm feeling very bored! Everyone is studying Physics 'coz they have a Physics exam on Monday. Everyone is learning new things but I'm not.

Yesterday I watched a very funny and meaningful show called *Mr Destiny*. It's 'bout a man, Larry, who regrets not hitting the ball in his baseball match years ago. He is not satisfied with his present life 'coz he thinks it could have been much better. Then he goes to this dark bar to drink. The man at the counter, Mike, is actually a magic man. After listening to his problems, Mike gives him a magic potion called Spilt Milk. Larry drinks it. When he leaves the bar, his life has actually changed (from the moment he hit the ball and married the prom queen) but he doesn't know it. So he goes back to his house but it's not his house anymore. His wife is different too. He later realizes that he doesn't have any friends even though he has a beautiful wife and lots of money. Finally he's able to go back to his real life and he's learned to treasure his life. Isn't life funny? If you make one decision, it leads to other events. Even one decision could change the rest of your life.

I've finished Lit. and History papers. Right now, I feel terrible and sad and everything.

BYE. I'll write when I'm in a better mood.
Love, Pei Yi

PS We played a trick on Lily Sim by writing a love letter to her, as if it's from a JC guy. We said, "I just love you to wear your orange-and-black dress. It brings out your femininity," and showered tons of praises on her. The next day, she wore that orange-and-black dress again! She seldom wore it before. But everyday, she wears white stockings. That *hiau po*!

Tuesday 20 October

Dear Mei Yee

The Lancome cosmetics company came to our school for a promotional session. They taught us how to clean our face and apply makeup. We get to try the cleansers out. Everything was so expensive! One tube of washing foam costs around S$40! But still, so many girls were ordering all that junk.

Love, Pei Yi

5
Sec 4 Now!

Saturday 2 January

Dear Mei Yee

Hi! I hope you have written to me already, no matter how boring it is in BM, as you say.

Jen Nee and I reached our hostel on 29 Dec. My new room this year is A320 and now Jen Nee is my roommate—yipee! And the only thing I can see of Eric's room is whether the light is on or not. I like this room. It is very cool and has a pretty good view.

The next day, 30 Dec, we met the Sec 1 Juniors at their Briefing. We were supposed to introduce ourselves and mix and mingle. I certainly didn't enjoy doing that. I guess I'm not a very good senior—certainly not one you'd look up to, like Alisa.

I saw Eric in the morning when Nancy and Eric discussed how much sugar paper to buy. You see, Eric is in charge of the Briefing deco. He's always in charge of things. The deco looked weird. The banner "ASEAN FOREVER" was done by several people and everyone cutting out a letter in his own style. So, letters of every imaginable style in fluorescent green were assembled. Eric's "A" wasn't even cut properly and it was already stuck there!

After shopping for essentials, I rearranged my room.

On the 31st, we met the Sec 3 Juniors (isn't it terrible to be Seniors). Elizabeth is wonderful and so natural when talking to them and their parents.

Oh ya, I'm very happy for Nicole—she did get her scholarship renewed for Sec 3. Remember last year she was in danger of losing it?

In the evening, we went to Orchard Road (both guys and girls). We came back only the next morning 'coz we wanted to celebrate New Year's Day.

We walked a lot, sat in a park and talked, ate and watched *A Few Good Men*. I was tongue-tied, nervous and hated myself for being so —— (I don't even know what word to use to describe this stupidity) because of Eric's presence. Sunny was so sociable. She is witty and funny and mixes very well with the guys.

Eric usually "commands" the guys. He is so popular with them and everyone does what he says. I walked beside him once but I screwed up the chance to talk to him. I was very nervous and wanted to think of witty remarks; instead I ended up saying stupid stuff. I'm never going to try to be witty again. Eric asked me why I wasn't with Jen Nee, he thought we're very close and always together. He also asked what room I'm in. I'd already checked what room he is in but I asked anyway. Then I asked, "You went to New Zealand?" He went with some Networking members and didn't have to pay a cent! He gave Nancy, Pau Leen and Nicole some souvenirs. Then he asked how I knew he went. I said, "Nancy told me you gave her a souvenir." And I hoped he did not misunderstand me to be hinting that I want one too because he said sorry, he didn't have enough souvenirs to give everyone!

In the park also, I sat beside him, but didn't say anything. Uggg. Why am I so terrible!? He just asked me whether I wanted his biscuits. And then later, because my lips were drying up, I asked whether he had water and I drank his orange juice.

Oh ya, he now wears contact lenses and new specs. I told him he looks more intellectual with his specs.

Oh dear, I hope you're not falling asleep with this brain-numbing boredom.

To continue, he is looking as cute as ever! When we ate at Long John Silver's he sat in front of me. We told some jokes. I hate speaking to many people at once, like when we're all in a group, because I'll get so nervous that I can't speak fluently. Guess I'm not made a public speaker!

At 5 am I was very sleepy. We were hanging around outside Orchard Cinema, playing games. I slept so that I could eschew obligations to talk. I asked Cheng Hoe whether he has Science jokes. You know that joke, "Why did the Koala Bear fall off the tree?" Cheng Hoe answered, "Gravity." He's so funny.

He's always saying Penang this, Penang that: "Are there any juniors from Penang?", "Look! Penang food."

On the night of 1 Jan, we took the Sec 3s to the hostel field and played games sitting in a circle. Eric was there.

Today is the 2nd. Jen Nee and I had KFC then shopped at Beauty World for groceries. When someone came up and said, "Give me your wallet!" I thought it was for real—turned out to be Matt, Cheng Hoe and ... (tadah!) Eric going for lunch! Unfortunately, we'd already eaten! Anyway, we talked for a while, then we went back. I haven't talked to Eric since.

Well, bye.
Love, Pei Yi

Sunday 3 January

Dear Mei Yee

Hi! Today, on an impulsive decision, I paged for Eric to ask him to lunch. Although I wanted to invite him only, I blurted out, "Jen Nee, Nicole and Sunny are going," and that he could bring his friends too. I was relieved when he said ok. I rushed back to Block A and begged Jen Nee, Nicole and Sunny to go too. It turned out that he brought a whole batch of guys, fifteen of them, and there were only four girls—me, Jen Nee, Nicole and Sunny. We ate at Beauty World. The guys didn't join us although they sat nearby, but Eric was obliged to sit beside me and walk beside me etc. Poor guy. He's so nice. The five of us sat in this arrangement:

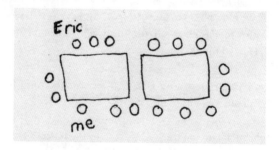

After lunch, we wanted to buy lacy panties for someone's birthday. Eric didn't know if he was supposed to come with us but was too polite to leave us. The other guys went their own way and Eric walked with us.

Actually, I don't know how to tell you how I feel about all this. It's not exactly what I want. I think, now, surely he knows that I like him, and being such a nice person, he's nice to me. That's all. I want to get my mind off this.

BYE.
Love Pei Yi

Monday 11 January

Dear Mei Yee

Yesterday, we went to ECP (East Coast Park) for Signature Hunt. It's an annual tradition but this time we are the seniors and we get to command the juniors to do embarrassing things. Well, actually we didn't have that many ideas of what we should tell them to perform.

Let me tell you all about Eric. At ECP, he was very cool in sunglasses. He really looks like the kind of rich-sociable-highclass-stylish men you see on adverts!! Eric asked a girl to propose to me. Later, I asked a guy to hold a conversation with him for two minutes while I stood and watched. After Signature Hunt, the rest played games but I was too lazy to join in so I sat on the beach with Alisa and Jen Nee. Gaik Teong came and talked to us. I think that Gaik Teong is very interesting and intelligent. He likes to tell people about things. He'll go, "Do you know what those black things are? They're snails," and he'll show them to you, and "These people are Filipinos" etc. You can learn a lot from him. He's funny too. I feel at ease with him but SO nervous with Eric.

Then I sat with Nancy under a tree. I was reading *The Merchant of Venice* when Eric came and sat beside me. He said he wanted to read too. Naturally, I couldn't concentrate and couldn't digest a single word. Then Nancy saw a caterpillar on the ground nearby and shrieked. She has been shrieking in shrill tones that assailed our ears the whole day, probably to get attention. Oops, I'm digressing from the topic. To continue my account of what happened, Nancy ran off shrieking, so it was just Eric and me under the tree. Eric asked whether I like to read and who my favourite authors are. I told him about Enid Blyton, Roald Dahl and Judy Blume. I asked him to tell me about his New Zealand trip. It seems that that is the only thing I can remember about him when he is around. He must think that I'm obsessed with New Zealand or something. Then his friends came and I didn't talk to him anymore. We went back after a while.

The most interesting thing I asked any of the juniors to do was for a girl and a guy to hold hands, accost some strangers near the beach and say to them, "We're getting married soon. Wish us luck." I also asked a pair of girls to do the same thing. It was interesting to see the strangers' reactions, like on *Candid Camera*!

At night, I was reading newspapers when Eric came to read newspapers too. I went over and asked him to give me $2 because I'm treasurer of our Batch and then I sat beside him. I couldn't think of things to talk to him at that time, so there we were, just reading newspapers in silence, except that I was very distracted and stared at a page for a long time and then I turned the page so that he wouldn't know that I wasn't really reading.

Love, Pei Yi

Sunday 31 January

Dear Mei Yee

Hi! It's been quite a while since I've written to you and such a lot has happened …

Last night, we went to CJC Hostel to give juniors signatures. I was sitting with Miriam (Sec 4, CHIJ) when Eric came to sit beside Miriam. Then he introduced himself to her and he asked her what school she was from. Miriam replied, "CHIJ". Eric said, "Oh, I was wondering why you are so close to Pei Yi. Won't Jen Nee be jealous?" I asked him, "Who are you close to?" and Miriam said, "She means, 'Do you have a girlfriend?'" "I mean, guys," I said. Eric replied, "No one in particular." For photography, I have to do this exercise and I want to ask Eric to be the subject the next time I see him.

I went to Chinatown to take photos yesterday. I wanted to take photos of people but it's rather difficult if you're not invisible. Old people have a taboo against photo-taking and might scream at you.

Oh ya, the other day, Jen Nee and I sang *Daniel* for the Karaoke contest. Actually we wanted *Daniel* by Wilson Phillips but found out too late that the laser disc's *Daniel* is sung by Elton John in orange sunglasses. The style is so different and horrible! Nancy and Nicole's *I Know Him So Well* was really good!

Did you enter the Commonwealth Essay Competition? I wrote an essay about music.

We had New Year celebration in school. Lion dance and mass. CHIJ girls really have this spirit of belonging and pride of the school. I don't really feel it 'coz I'm not close to my classmates but I think, if I'd come in Sec 1, I'd probably have it too. If I'd come in Sec 1, I'd probably not have chosen A4 class. Anyway, I'm glad that I'll be able to leave my class at the end of the year. I feel that people who are "normal" and easy to talk to are those in Science classes, in other words, the more decent ones. I can't stand rowdy people.

I really hope to get good results so that I can go to RJC. And I really want to get more scholarships so that my parents don't have to spend so much hard-earned money to send me to England.

The other day, I was reading *The Chinese Culture* in the library and I realized that I'm so ignorant about my own culture! Everything looked so foreign to me. I didn't even know that the Chinese way of counting the age of someone also includes the time of gestation; i.e. once you're born you're already one year old. In fact last year, I said to Jen Nee, "Hey, we are actually older 'coz we spend nine months in our mother's stomach."

I finished reading *The Irish Question*, which is about the Catholics in Northern Ireland wanting to be part of Ireland and the Protestants (Unionists) in Northern Ireland wanting to be part of UK. They feel threatened by each other as Ireland and Northern Ireland have more Catholics whereas in Northern Ireland only, the Protestants outnumber the Catholics. What I don't get is why people always separate into religious groups. Why not separate into "Those Who Like Singing" and "Those Who Hate Singing," or anything else??

Do you know which part of China your ancestors were from? Were your grandparents born in China?

Eric gave many girls weird Chinese New Year cards. Some with ten-cent coins or batteries stuck on them. Jen Nee and I gave him one that has red dots on the outside, and on the inside, it says "If a sexy person opens this card, the blue dots in front will turn red" but we wrote that the card is spoilt and he'll have to let us check whether he's sexy some other time. The other day, I met him in the office and he asked me whether I want to check then. I said "No"!!

Reply SOON.
Love, Pei Yi

Wednesday 10 February

Dear Mei Yee
Hi! Received your letter last week. Have you received mine (the pink one)?

Yesterday was a great day, although it didn't start so well 'coz Jen Nee and I woke up late. Nevertheless, we still went to school. The wonderful events culminated with a nice time talking to Eric. That was what made me so happy. Let me tell you all about it.

Our warden–group meeting was just over. Nicole came to tell me that Eric was reading newspapers upstairs so I went to read too. But even though I sat very near, within talking distance, I did not say anything other than "Hi". Later he began talking to some guys so I left after reading the newspaper.

Back in my room, I was feeling regretful because I didn't have any conversation starters whenever an opportunity presented itself. So I went down again and was very lucky that he was standing in line, waiting to phone. So I decided to phone my parents and got in line behind him.

I like talking to him very much. I found out that his father is a doctor and his mother helps his father at the clinic. He's an only child, and he likes his class in RI. He also likes living in the hostel because he has many friends to do stuff with. I asked him if he gets depressed a lot and he said not much. Wow, he sounds like a very positive person who is able to make the best out of every situation. I wanted to tell him about my Arts and Science class predicament but didn't because I didn't want to sound like a negative person. I didn't appear nervous, I think. In a nutshell, I was very pleased after that. Oh ya, when I was talking to him, I was trying to remember what I had read in *The Fine Art of Flirting* book.

The Fine Art of Flirting says that people who are good at flirting are not considered flirts by others because they do it so naturally. People just think that they're friendly and interesting. The suggestions given by the book are:

1 Carry something unusual so that it will become a conversation piece
2 Enter a room with style
3 Dress well even when going grocery shopping (people in the hostel always walk around with T-shirts, shorts and slippers so that would be weird)
4 Show interest in him

Love, Pei Yi

Friday 12 February

Dear Mei Yee
Hi! Our Orientation is in a week's time (20 Feb)! I think our item is

going to be very impressive and interesting. The girls are doing a unique tribal dance to the song *Free Your Mind* and the guys are doing a kung fu dance to a Chinese New Year song. We're supposed to be two antagonistic tribes and then we end with a song *In The Still of The Night*. Do you know it? I am so pleased with it 'coz the four parts sound terrific in a cappella. We divided ourselves into four groups and I taught them "Shu dup shu bi du." The song is ringing in my head now.

Do you notice that my letters are now very short compared with last year's? I think it's because I've lost my dependency on you and don't feel the need to tell you every little petty thing now—that is good. I mean, we're still best friends but I don't have an unhealthy dependence on you anymore.

Next Saturday is Prize-giving Day. I'm getting 3rd prize for Science. It's rather silly 'coz I hardly know anything about Science. This Hong Kong scholar in 4S2 is really great. Guess how many prizes she's getting. Five! 1st for Physics, 3rd for Add. Maths, Highly Commended for E. Maths, Highly Commended for Geography and 3rd for Chemistry. Jen Nee is getting 1st prize for History. I feel so jealous 'coz everyone is so wonderfully clever.

Right now, I'm feeling quite terrible because I feel that everyone is good at this and that and I'm not.
Love, Pei Yi

Saturday 20 February

Dear Mei Yee
I just returned from Orientation. Eric slow-danced with me! I'm elated but not as much as I thought I'd be. Still, I'm very happy. The fast dance session was very long and boring and it was sweltering in the RGS hall so I stayed in the classroom with Jen Nee and a few others for quite some time. Then I went back to the hall. It was slow dance so I danced with Jen Nee. Then Eric came and asked if he could take over so I put my

arms around his neck and he put his hands on my waist. I can't remember what song it was. I asked him how come he's not involved in our performance and we talked about the performance. Nothing interesting, really, but I was glad that we actually talked like friends. I mean, we're not good friends yet, but every conversation is progress in the right direction!

Then he said I have a very small waist but he guessed it's alright for a girl. I said it's not small for a girl. He said, "You mean there are smaller ones?" That's about all I can remember. The song ended and he said, "Thank you" and left.

Love, Pei Yi

Sunday 21 February

Hi Mei Yee
I'm still very happy about Eric. Maybe he asked me because he is so nice and polite and he knows that I like him, but I don't care whether he likes me or not right now. I want us to become good friends. Well, actually slow-dancing is not such a great thing after all.
Love, Pei Yi

Wednesday 24 March (*Back from hols!*)

Dear Mei Yee
Hi! I figured I won't be receiving a letter from you if I didn't write first so I'm writing now. Lucky you, a whole week of hols. We only have one day off for Hari Raya—tomorrow.

I think if I see Eric again now after not seeing him during the holidays, we can probably talk for longer periods of time compared to before and maybe eventually become good friends! I've decided not to be so focused on getting a boyfriend but just enjoy friendships with guys. Eric is a good start! Yay.

Well, actually I don't have anything else to write. My daily concerns are school, reading books and eating. The usual, and I enjoy it. Well, actually I don't really enjoy lessons with my class but never mind. I'm looking forward to a good JC next year, and if you come, it'd be perfect! That's all.

Bye and reply SOON.
Love, Pei Yi
PS I hope your letter is not shorter than this miserably short one.

Sunday 4 April

Dear Mei Yee
Hi! I was very glad to receive your letter.

Nowadays, I'm becoming more and more tense and must-not-waste-time. If I don't spend my time doing something constructive, I'll feel terrible.

Yesterday I went to Orchard Road with Jen Nee 'coz I needed to buy a filter for my camera and also I was looking for sports shoes. I couldn't find comfortable and beautiful sports shoes within my price budget so I decided not to buy any yet.

Have you heard of Bram Stokers' *Dracula*? It's rated R(A). We watched it secretly last week at our batch-inning but we didn't have time to finish it so on Friday we watched it again. We had to lock the door of the karaoke room and be secretive. The videotape belongs to Betty. Such was our luck that Ms Lily Sim (remember her?) came in suddenly, swinging her key. Matt, who had his finger on the controls, at once stopped the show. The trouble-loving Ms Lily Sim immediately suspected that something fishy was going on and stood there watching so we had to play the tape. There were actually no dirty scenes. It was R(A) 'coz it was quite gory. Well, there were one or two nude scenes but they're hardly erotic. Anyway, Ms Lily Sim wanted to jump on every opportunity to make trouble so she called Mr Goh (a very nice, innocent-looking man working at the hostel office) to see it. Mr Goh watched for a few minutes and then said that nothing was wrong.

Nevertheless, Ms Lily Sim wouldn't let us off so easily. She asked severely, "Who brought this tape in?" Of course we couldn't say it belonged to Betty. She wanted us to hand it over for inspection after the show. They got so worried about it, "What if they tell MOE?" and made up some tales to tell. But, when I handed Ms Lily Sim the tape, she said, no need already. She just wanted to show her authority at that time. She probably doesn't even know it's R(A). I think it's 'coz we knew it was R(A) and we felt guilty and afraid at that moment that she was able to make a big deal out of it. Our subconscious minds attracted trouble and her subconscious mind, always on the look out for trouble, found a chance for her to flex her muscles.

Have you been keeping yourself up to date on the world news? Korea is building a nuclear weapons plant and they have resigned from the Nuclear Non-Proliferation Treaty! And do you know about Boris Yeltsin? I don't really know about him. Brandon Lee (son of Bruce Lee, whoever he was) died when a supposedly empty gun fired a bullet into him.

Oh ya, I haven't finished talking about my birthday. I was very glad to receive many books 'coz I wanted books.

These are what people gave me:

Angela, Jen Nee and Nicole—a book: *Four Great American Classics*
Lingling and Huiwee—a pencilcase and a letter-writing kit including a set of stamps!
Yoonphaik—a dictionary and a bible
Nancy, Alisa—a book: *General Knowledge*; two Ziggy comics
A history book and a white blouse for me from me

My happy birthday was really consummated when I received a birthday card from Eric. It was a paper bird and he wrote Happy Birthday. It's just a piece of folded paper but I was really head over heels with delight.

You know, many of the scholars are really high achievers. Matt got 1st in a Physics Quiz for every school in Singapore! We celebrated his victory at Denny's. Actually the girls didn't want to go as we don't really like Matt but Cheng Hoe persuaded us so much that we did. Elizabeth is always winning British Council debates. We went on the day before my birthday so they sang me a birthday song and Cheng Hoe bought me ice cream and put a candle on it.

Elizabeth is a really good flirt. Not flirt as in *hiau* and cheap but flirt as in has many guy friends, as described in the book *The Fine Art of Flirting*. So, now we seldom mix with her as she finds more time for guys. Sometimes she's *zhong se ching you* (cares about the opposite sex more than friends).

Elizabeth is starting to pair up with Roger. Alisa is finding her right man in Marcus, a JC guy who is also interested in her, of course. I think he's about the only admirer whom she likes, from her lorry loads of admirers.
Love, Pei Yi

Thursday 9 April

Dear Mei Yee
How are you? What have you been doing? Do write to me if you can spare the time!

Did I tell you about the time Mr Como was very cross 'coz I was taking bad, boring photographs? It was of Jen Nee and Nicole, but I had not planned beforehand and did not think properly before I took the shots. Of course, I ended up with terrible shots that looked like "happy holiday shots". Mr Como gave me an hour-long lecture about how I'm not using my head and applying what I know. The next day, he said he was sorry for being so harsh. On Saturday, he took me and Jen Nee to Toa Payoh Central to take photographs. I've to develop The Eye. Mr Como said my photos are improving but they still have a long way to go.

I made a birthday card for my mother using photographic paper. I put it under a nice picture, cut out the lettering and put it on top to expose it. I got quite a nice effect. Photography's a lot of fun, but not at all easy. Our Malay Prelims were just over—two days ago. Everyone was sleeping and yawning after one hour but we still had half an hour left.

Anyway, I really have to study now. Do you have mid-year exams? We only have exams for Accounts, E. Maths and Add. Maths.

Do reply.
Love, Pei Yi

Friday 20 May

Dear Mei Yee
At last I've received your letter! I was so glad—I can't believe you accumulated the pages for over a month!

Congrats for passing your driving test. I can't believe you can actually drive now! It's really a transition into adulthood, isn't it? I can't even ride a motorbike.

I can't believe I'm already seventeen! I feel that I'm still such an ignorant, silly, immature girl who hardly knows anything. And in JC and all the subsequent years, I'll probably only be learning commerce, commerce, commerce, so I'll stay ignorant forever about lots of things that I wish to know. I can't imagine how some people can drop out of school and go to work at our age!!!!!!! At this age, my knowledge is just a speck of sand in the deserts of knowledge and learning in this world.

I'm doing the Accounts exam after hols. Both Maths exams were quite easy. I was very lucky in Add. Maths 'coz for a proving question $\sec2 x + \cos2 x_- = \sec2x$ (or something like that) $1 + 2\sin x \cos x$ I couldn't get it so I left it. Then before the two and a half hours were up, I thought that I might as well write some rubbish and then suddenly from the rubbish, I saw the answer! So I quickly wrote it properly— seconds before the time was up. I made lots and lots of careless mistakes but luckily I corrected them. Nevertheless, there might be some undiscovered ones. I was rather pleased with how I did. I'm still waiting for the results.

The JC scholarships have just been given away. Betty was very sad not to get one, while about 60 "old" scholars did get them. I said "But it's only S$3,000", but Betty said it's the prestige. Also, it'll be easier to get other scholarships next time. All the scholars are such super-achievers. Just to name a few: Eric is President of the Networking Club, Matt is President of Student Council, Pau Leen is President of Canoeing Club, Sunny is President of Volleyball, Ekan is President of Fencing Club, Cheng Hoe is President of Physics Club, Elizabeth is President of Literature Society and History Society, Nancy is President of Choir, Alisa is class prefect … (the list goes on).

Well, I guess the only way to be happy is to let go of all wants and desires and be satisfied with your life and make the best out of what you have. That's all. I shall end this letter here.
Love, Pei Yi

Friday 21 May

Dear Mei Yee
Betty has been quite depressed because she did not get a JC scholarship. She will go back to Malaysia to continue pre-university instead of going to a JC in Singapore. Well, at least she won't be in a *kiasu* environment anymore.
Love, Pei Yi

Sunday 27 June

Dear Mei Yee

Hi! I just came back from BM. I came back by plane. The bus journey from the airport to the hostel was twice as long as the plane journey!

Yesterday, I ate so much. My mum made shark's fin soup and throughout the day, I was stuffing myself with potato chips, milk, rice, veg, meat etc.

I phoned you last night to wish you good luck for the 1119 exam but you were out. So GOOD LUCK and have confidence if this reaches you before your exam. Tell me all 'bout it!

Yesterday I was in front of the TV the whole day! I watched *Wild and Crazy Kids*, *Kid's Court* (wonderful show), Cantonese serials, *Beyond Reality*, *Beverly Hills*, *Full House* and other insignificant shows. *Beyond Reality* is really exciting. Have you even watched it? It's on every week. Oh, did you watch *When He's Not A Stranger*? It's about a girl who was raped by a popular guy who is a jerk in a medical college. It was good (the show I mean).

Do you notice that we never see dead animals in nature? Not the ones like cats and dogs knocked down by cars but those that die naturally. I'm sure hundreds of animals, like birds, lizards, cockroaches, mosquitoes and bugs die each day but we never see them dead, only alive. I read an article 'bout it. I didn't notice it myself. The writer said that if a herd of elephants comes across a dead elephant, they will carry it around until a suitable hiding place is found. If they meet an elephant skeleton, they will carry a few bones each and hide them carefully.

Jen Nee registered for TOEFL exam (English test if you want to go to the USA) and my dad says he'll let me take it too so I'm going to, in August. Well, I'd better sleep now.
Love, Pei Yi

Thursday 22 July

Dear Mei Yee

Hi! I was so glad to receive your letter! It's been so long since I'd written to you—I'm gonna have to write a long letter and wrack my brains about which events I haven't told you yet.

Recently, it was Eric's birthday. Jen Nee and I made him a card in the darkroom, using photographic paper. We wrote, "We gave you an unconventional card 'coz you're an unconventional person."

Did I even tell you my new form teacher is a pretentious hypocrite? She's always trying to be so nice! She also flirts with the new male teachers in school! But none of the students like or respect her. "Girls, I want to have a good rapport with you. The Sec 1 girls and I get along very well together. They tell me everything ..." She can't teach Lit at all! She just reads from the book, tells us things we already know and she gets her own facts and characters mixed up! She also likes to boast: "Girls, I was a runner in the university. I got third place once" or "Girls, I actually learnt Science before; I switched to Arts only later."

And she made a horrible mistake when explaining a story we were reading, the people dug a trench and burnt the grass around the trench to stop a forest fire spreading and she told us, "It's to use up the oxygen there. When there's no more oxygen, the fire can't continue burning."!

I'm taking TOEFL. I've sent the form and the RM98 bank draft.

I used to be a terrible busybody and envy those who have a lot of gossip and know about what's happening but now I'm not anymore. Jen Nee made me realize that knowing all the gossip does not make you happier.

Jen Nee and I went to Metro to buy clothes for Farewell. I bought a white sleeveless blouse quite some time ago 'coz it was only S$6.90. There were sales at Metro and I bought these:

1 A long blue skirt with buttons running down the front for S$33
2 A black jacket for S$29. This is a real bargain. Jackets usually cost a hundred odd. (This is for the executive scene. I could have borrowed from someone I guess, but this was such a bargain!)
3 A dark blue tight-skirt to go with the jacket

I was so excited about all these new clothes 'coz they're really nice.

Jen Nee bought a long skirt too for S$43 and a black blouse for S$33. Hers weren't on sale. She actually also wanted my blue skirt but I saw the skirt first, you see.

What do you mean "The elephants are so cute"? Did I tell you anything about elephants? Oh! Is it about their bones? Now I remember!

Singapore really has a lot of acronyms. How many do you recognize? AJC, SJI, NJC, MRT, RJC, GST, TGIW, HDB, RGS, SBC, MCQ, MGS, SBS, COE, CHIJ, TGIF, KFC.

I think books influence me very easily. I always believe what I read. Jen Nee says next time, if she wants to trick me, she'll publish something in a book so I'll read and believe it.

After reading an article about how crazy it is that some parts of the earth starve while other parts get diseases from overeating, I wrote a petition about letting us take our own food instead of being served the huge portions by the canteen people, as we waste three dustbins of food every dinner. I got people to sign it then asked Nicole to pass it to the Sec 3s but the stupid boys lost it. I wrote another one, and this time, I'm gonna make sure that I keep it properly.

Well, I think I'll stop now. I'll write to you again after Farewell.

REPLY SOON!
Love, Pei Yi

PS Alisa has a bf already—Marcus from Penang. He's in NJC. They don't act like a couple in the hostel, though, only outside!

Monday 9 August

Dear Mei Yi

Singapore has its own *Candid Camera*-style show called *Gotcha*. It's really funny! I like watching the local setting. In one episode, the *Gotcha* host pretended to speak a foreign language to unsuspecting strangers, "Blob blob blob? Blob blob …" as if they're asking directions to somewhere. A woman who was eating at a coffee shop pretended to know the blob blob language. "Blob blob", she said, pointing into the distance just to get rid of the blob blob guy pestering her!

Love, Pei Yi

Wednesday 11 August

Dear Mei Yee

Jen Nee did something very silly last week. She was walking alone in Orchard Road when a young man approached her. Stammering and stuttering incoherently, he plunged into a long, confusing story about losing his wallet in a taxi and having no money to take a taxi to East Coast where he lives. He claimed that the taxi sped away before he could take his wallet. Isn't it stupid? Well, Jen Nee was so confused, and didn't have time to think properly. Finally, she said, "So you want to borrow money, is it?" The man said yes, but he wants to see whether his friend is in Denny's or not first. Jen Nee went with him and he came out from Denny's, saying his friend was not in.

Jen Nee offered to lend him S$10 but he said East Coast is too far, he needed at least S$20. He assured her that he would return the money and jotted down her address (wow, he conveniently had a pen right there and then). As you would have guessed by now, the man was a con man! He left with S$20 and later Jen Nee began to wonder how she could have believed such a fishy story.

I could hardly believe such a remarkable incident! Jen Nee felt very angry with herself for being so gullible. I felt angry with the cunning man. He definitely has his strategies:

1 Approach young teenagers walking alone (lone people are easy to convince; Jen Nee looks very "blur" sometimes)
2 Talk incoherently to confuse her
3 Convince her you're telling the truth by appearing to look for your friend first
4 Write down the victim's address

Who in the right mind would borrow money from a stranger to take a taxi? I was shocked that such stories could actually fool people. I bet he earns quite a sum cheating people everyday.

Anyway, the next time I meet a stranger who wants to borrow money to take a taxi, I'll say: "Borrow from someone else", "I don't have any money" or "Take a bus!"

Jen Nee and I were so *geram* that we acted out the scene again and we changed the ending to her punching the guy.
Love, Pei Yi

Thursday 12 August

Dear Mei Yee
I just finished reading your letter. I notice that I usually receive your letters on Thursdays! I cannot resist the temptation to write to you straightaway.

I got my Malay 2 results last week. Guess what? I got C3! Terrible, isn't it? I was quite shocked myself 'coz I'm a Malaysian.

Jen Nee got A1 in Malay. Nancy, whose Malay has always been the best among us all, surprisingly received a C3 too. She cried like crazy. So did

Alisa 'coz she got C4. She was hysterical, I heard. I know I always think mean things of Alisa about her being *kiasu* and pretending not to study, but when I realize that she probably also feels insecure about her own intelligence, I feel a bit sorry for her.

Thank goodness I get to take the exam again in November! This taught me a lesson, not to be over-confident. I'm starting to read Malay books to improve my Malay. Sometimes I can't even bring to mind simple Malay words like *melarang* or *tegas*. My essays sound like a Primary School kid's.

I wasn't all that sad about C3 'coz it's just Malay. If it had been Maths or English, I would have cried but I was wondering how I'm going to tell my parents, as I'm usually saying to them that Malay here is very easy. Surprisingly, they weren't angry or disappointed about it. My dad was hoping that I was not too disappointed over it.

We just had a whole stretch of hols 'coz of National Day (9 August). Friday (6/8) was Mass and celebrations in school so I skipped school. Mon—the real National Day. Tuesday—holiday but I wasted it 'coz I suffered great pain from period cramps. I thought that my period pains had ceased for good but they just reoccurred this month.

The year is going to be over soon, isn't it? I wonder where everyone will be, say, six months from now.

I have the same feeling as you—I feel that I've not grabbed many opportunities in my life so far and there're many things I won't be able to experience once I'm past my youth. It's a rather sad thought.

Yesterday I was very happy 'coz my recent two rolls of films produced excellent results. It was of Jen Nee having a cocktail in Dynasty restaurant.

Next week, Jen Nee and I are putting together a photographic exhibition in school and I've more than enough prints to choose from. Good prints really please me. I can't wait to enlarge them properly. I can send them for O levels but Mr Como expects me to take even more photos. He said, "Now that you're on the springboard, are you going to walk on and leap or just walk away contented?"

Maybe I'll take more photos after prelims (starting 24/8).

Friday 3 September

Dear Mei Yi

Received a postcard from Betty who's in a twinning college in KL. She'll continue her course at an American college. She's quite happy in KL and thinks that her not getting the JC scholarship was a blessing in disguise. Actually she'll be going to a pretty good college in America even without going through all the stress of JC here. I wonder what the point it sometimes in all this intense competition for JC places in Singapore.

The hostel barbecue was fun. The JC guys entertained us throughout with their band performance. Marcus (Alisa's bf) wanted to dedicate a song to Alisa but he was too shy to say it! He stuttered, "To ... er ..." and the crowd shouted, "Who? Who?" Marcus hesitated, then said, "to everybody ...". "Hey!" the crowd teased. "... And to my Princess!" he finally managed! (So romantic, huh?)

We were divided into groups according to our warden groups and each group had three pits and chicken wings, sausages and corn. I had fun roasting the marshmallows but I didn't eat them 'coz they were too sweet. I voiced out, "How come the inside melts but the surface doesn't?" and Niles, whom I no longer have a crush on but still think he's very cute, answered my question. Eric was actually in another group but he came to talk to me. I can't really remember what we talked about. It was casual and quite nice. Oh ya, I asked him if he wanted to be the "model" for my photo project and he said OK. I told him it's not for nude photos. Ha! Ha! We're going to Orchard Road this weekend to buy

173

some props for the photoshoot. Maybe I can buy myself some makeup and ask Nancy to do a makeover for me then ask Eric to take a picture of me. Actually it's nice to be friends with him without having a crush on him. I can be myself and not worry about what I say. In fact, I'm even quite witty sometimes! I think I'm finally learning something from *The Fine Art of Flirting*. I must recommend it to any shy juniors in the future.

Ms Lily Sim was also at the barbecue, and she smiled at Jen Nee and me. Maybe she's not that bad after all, and it's us who are *kolot* to think that she's flirting with the JC guys. Or maybe all this happiness about Eric is making me all softhearted and love everyone.

Saturday 4 September

Dear Mei Yee
Hi, I received your letter a few days ago. I waited for a few days for my exams to be over.

Now the one-week hols are beginning and after hols, we have exams again. However, most of my studying subjects are over. I just finished History today. Yippee! My hand and fingers were dying while I was writing the five essays.

Learning History essays can be such a bore. Thank goodness Jen Nee also takes History, so we can discuss and motivate each other. We acted out some parts, and laughed and laughed. She is always the native ruler; I am the Dutchman or Bugis.

Hey, only three more months and the school year will be over, and I'll be going to a good JC in Singapore, hopefully! Well, I don't know if I got into the JCs that I applied to yet, but whichever one I go to, I'll be choosing Science subjects. I'll get to learn Physics finally! I'm so excited that you may be coming to Singapore too! JC will be better because it will be co-ed, so I'll have more normal friendships with guys! I'm really looking forward to all these new things! As you know, I always think back and recap my progress over the past year. These are my thoughts for the year so far, compared with last year.

Good changes:

1 I don't read dirty books anymore! I just outgrew them for some odd reason. Maybe because there are real things to do in my life instead of just reading silly fantasies!
2 I gossip less.
3 I'm nicer to people in the hostel who are less confident or people who need friends, like Nicole.
4 I can talk to guys normally now.
5 Eric and I may become friends who actually hang out together. Maybe!
6 I'm not so obsessed with crushes now. Will try not to have any more until I actually know the guy well.
7 I'm more sociable now, and have many friends in the hostel. I'm less dependent on you now. (That's good, right?)
8 I'm very happy that Jen Nee and me are such good friends!

Things that I still need to change:

1 I am still quite *kiasu* and competitive!
2 I get very impatient when things are not going the most efficient way possible or if I'm not being efficient. I hate wasting time.

Actually, I think I would probably be less *kiasu* if I wasn't living and studying in this *kiasu* environment. It's hard not to be *kiasu* when everyone around you is. However, deep down, I still know what really matters in life—family, friends and being a good person—and I don't really care if I am the top student or if I have a high-flying career in the future. So maybe I'm not truly *kiasu* but just ambitious!
Love, Pei Yi